Bathroom Access Denied

1

Jill looked at her watch to see that soon her friends would be coming to pick her up to go to the movies. They were celebrating the fact that they were all starting a new job tomorrow working at that place that handled all sorts of orders for swimming and other aquatic equipment.

Knowing that her friends would be arriving any minute Jill decided that she would go to the bathroom. Jill always made sure to go to the bathroom before leaving home as a precaution because she never knew when the next bathroom visit would be. Of course when she got to the movie theater she would probably go to the bathroom again before the movie started, again just as a precaution.

After going to the bathroom Jill heard that her friends were already beeping the car horn outside, so she figured that she had better get moving because he didn't want to keep everybody waiting, especially because if they knew she was keeping them waiting because she was going to the bathroom they would probably give her hell for it.

Jill ran out to the car and squeezed into the back seat with Leah and Patricia. In the front passenger seat was Ashley and in the driver's seat was Henry. The nearest movie theater was a half hour away so they made sure to leave good and early so that they would get good seats.

Everybody went over to the concession stand and got something but Jill decided that she would get the large popcorn and the really large soda.

"Are you sure you want to get a large soda like that," Leah said as she sort of smirked. "You know that you'll be running to the bathroom after all of that."

"I can sit through a movie without having to get up to go to the bathroom," Jill said.

"Yeah but the second that the movie is out you will be bolting for the bathroom!" Henry said as he laughed.

"Well of course, the movie is like three hours and that's not even considering the 20 minutes of previews before that!" Jill said shaking her head as they all got into the movie theater and took their seats.

Jill quickly finished her popcorn and soon started going to town on that soda. By about two hours into the movie she was definitely feeling a bit full in the bladder area, but she knew that she could wait until the end of the movie without it being a major problem. As soon as the credits started rolling Jill was practically ready to bolt.

"Where are you rushing off to?" Ashley said. "Don't you remember this is a Marvel movie, they always have more stuff after the credits."

"Oh right, I forgot," Jill said as she sat down and crossed her legs trying to be as subtle as possible. As the credits slowly crawled Jill had to admit that she was getting antsier. Standing up for a moment sort of fooled her bladder into thinking that relief was imminent, but now that they had to wait for about another 10 minutes of credits she was once again getting really antsy. But finally the credits finished up and there was nothing after them.

"I guess because it's the end of the first phase of movies they didn't have any previews at the end," Ashley said. "But hey it's better than that time that we waited at the end of that other movie and Captain America lectured us on having patience."

"But we were waiting patiently for all of that for nothing!" Jill said as she stood up.

"Let's wait for everyone to clear out so that we don't get stampeded upon as we are trying to get out of the theater," Patricia said.

They all noticed that Jill was doing that telltale sign where she was bending at the knees and put her hands on her knees.

"Jill's gotta pee!" Henry said as he began laughing.

"Announce it to the whole world why don't you!" Jill said as she danced around in place.

"Okay, hey everyone Jill has to pee!" Henry shouted and

laughed.

"Come on let's go, we have to beat the rush to the bathroom!" Jill said as she hit Henry in the arm and looked towards the back of the theater to see everybody stampeding out.

"I don't know, I think that we can just wait for everyone to get out," Leah said enjoying seeing the fact that Jill was practically begging.

"Guys this isn't funny!" Jill said. "This is why I prefer to sit in the aisle seat!"

"I disagree, I think this is pretty hilarious," Ashley said as everyone started laughing.

"You guys are such assholes!" Jill said as she stomped her feet.

"You know I tease her but I think Jill's right, I think I do need to use the bathroom myself," Ashley said as she started running towards the back of the theater. Luckily everyone else sitting to the right of Ashley had already left the movie theater giving her a clear beeline towards the back of the movie theater.

"Come on guys, let me through!" Jill said.

"I don't know how you could use those disgusting public toilets," Patricia said shaking her head.

"I don't know how you can go the entire day without using the bathroom!" Jill shouted. "Now come on and let me through! Either let me through I'm going to push my way through."

"Okay hold your horses Jill," Leah said. "And I suppose hold your bladder as well!"

"Ha ha, very funny, now move!" Jill said as the three of them very slowly, intentionally very slowly, walked out into the aisle as Jill started bolting into the hallway.

Jill quickly ran down the hallway bolting into the lobby which she thought was surprisingly full. That was when she noticed that the movie they were seeing was playing on four screens simultaneously and all of them were getting out at the same time.

"No no no!" Jill said as she started running up the stairs to where the bathrooms were. The line was basically snaking down the stairway.

Jill stood there infuriated as her three friends started walking up the stairs.

"Oh don't tell me that this is the freaking line," Leah said as she laughed.

"But it's not funny; this is all your fault for delaying me getting out of the movies!" Jill said. "You know how these multiplexes are all very crowded and more so if they have all of the movies getting out at once. You deliberately delayed me."

"Once again I have to disagree Jill, I think that this is quite funny," Henry said. "Well you're going to be here a while, I guess I will go use the men's room quickly as those sodas really do go right through you!"

"I hate you guys so much!" Jill said as she stood there dancing in line. "Holy crap I really have to pee!"

"Well at least it's not holy crap you have to crap," Leah said as she laughed.

"Can you at least see if Ashley is towards the front of the line, maybe she could let me cut or something?" Jill said as she crossed her legs grabbed onto the banister.

"Okay I'll go look," Patricia said.

"Thank you," Jill said as she grimaced and stuck out her tongue.

"This is why you shouldn't rely so much on public toilets," Leah said. "There's no reason why you can't wait until you get home to go to the bathroom."

"Not all of us have bladders of steel!" Jill said as she danced in place. "I really wish I had gone to the bathroom before the movie. I probably haven't gone in nearly 4 hours now and I had that huge soda!"

"Nobody told you to have a huge soda though."

"Yeah but when I'm eating popcorn like that I get thirsty, obviously."

"Well then I guess you have to deal with the consequences, at least you are keeping us entertained."

"Glad you find my predicament so entertaining!"

Of course Jill couldn't be too mad at them. Sure right now she was totally furious, but she knew that they loved seeing women desperate to go to the bathroom just as much as she did, she just resented the fact that she was pretty much always the one getting desperate all the time, and she frequently envied the bladder capacity of her friends.

"Wow you haven't even moved up more than a step or two I don't think," Henry said as he came back smiling.

"Well that was quick!" Jill said as she stuck out her tongue.

"And now you're going to lecture me on how much easier it is for men to go to the bathroom," Henry said.

"Well come on, it obviously is!" Jill said. "Look at this line, you didn't have to wait in this line!"

Henry shook his head. "Well if the line was this long I probably would just hold it until we get home."

"Yeah that would be the easiest option," Leah said.

"I didn't see any sign of Ashley," Patricia said.

"She wasn't waiting in line?" Jill asked.

Patricia shook her head. "I guess she must have beaten the crowds."

"Freaking figures!" Jill said as she bent at the knees a little bit.

"Hey guys," Ashley said as she came over and looked at Jill in line. "Holy crap this is where you are in line?" Ashley couldn't help but laughing.

"How did you manage to go so fast?!" Jill said.

Ashley smiled. "I guess I'm just quick, plus I managed to beat all of the crowds getting out of the other movie theater. If you had ran a little faster maybe you would have beaten the crowd as well."

"Well maybe if some people had gotten out of the movie theater faster I would have!" Jill said as she looked angrily at Leah, Patricia and Henry.

"Well you have quite a line in front of you," Ashley said with a smirk.

"How bad is it?" Jill said. "I'm almost afraid to ask."

Ashley whistled. "It's bad girl, it's bad."

"How bad is bad? I'm almost afraid to ask again, how many people were inside the bathroom?"

Ashley laughed. "Well you know I didn't stop to count or

anything like that but it's pretty damn packed in there. There has gotta be at least a couple of dozen women in the bathroom itself."

"I can't believe that you managed to beat the rush!" Jill said shaking her head before turning to Leah, Patricia and Henry. "This is all your fault! How many people are waiting outside the bathroom?"

"I didn't count them either, but hey I suppose I have nothing better to do now," Ashley said as she scampered off smiling and now standing outside of the line surveying everything.

Jill stood there still holding onto the banister and about a minute or two later Ashley pushed her way through the crowd and came back.

"Do you want to guess?" Ashley said with a wide smirk on her face.

"Judging by the look on your face I probably don't," Jill said.

"Well you're right about that," Ashley said as she laughed. "I'm not going to tell you the number unless you guess first? Hey it will kill some time."

"I want to be optimistic but I'm going to be pessimistic and guess like 20 or 25."

Ashley raised her hand above her head.

"Higher?" Jill said with a frown. "30?"

Ashley raised her hand even higher.

"Higher than 30!" Jill shouted. "35?"

Ashley raised her hand a little bit higher.

"Oh my God, 40?" Jill asked.

"38," Ashley said. "But I'm guessing that by now maybe one or two more people have got ahead in line, so you know be optimistic!"

"Fuck!" Jill said as she danced in place.

"But there's no need for potty mouth Jill, just because you have potties on the brain," Leah said.

"Ha potty!" Ashley said.

"I'm glad that you're all finding this so funny and amusing!" Jill said as she continued to shift around in place.

"Don't be a hypocrite, you know that if situations were reversed you would find it just as amusing to see one of us in a situation like that," Ashley said.

"That is 100% true, but the fact remains is that I am the one in the situation right now!" Jill said as she stuck her tongue out.

"I know, sucks for you," Ashley said as she laughed.

"Just try not to think about it, just try not to think about it," Jill said.

"About what, how badly you have to pee," Henry said as he laughed.

"Yes that!" Jill said.

"Oh my God is this the line," another woman said as she came over.

"Yep," Patricia said.

"Well forget that," the woman said as she walked away.

"But I really have to go!" her friend said.

"It'd be easier to go home," the other woman said as she dragged her friend away complaining.

"I think that they probably have the right idea," Patricia said.

"Yeah honestly," Leah said as she nodded in agreement.

"So should we get out of here?" Ashley said.

"Sounds like a good idea," Henry said.

"Wait a minute!" Jill shouted.

"What's the matter Jill," Ashley said.

"What's the matter is that I did not get to go to the bathroom yet!" Jill said.

"Well let's do this democratically, who thinks that we should just leave and wait until we get home," Leah said.

Everyone but Jill raised their hands.

"Wait a minute!" Jill shouted as she crossed and uncrossed her legs. "The needs of my bladder are not affected by a democratic vote!"

"It is kind of realistic though Jill," Patricia said. "This is going to be a pretty long line and it would probably be quicker if we just drove home."

"Are you crazy?!" Jill shouted. "It's rush hour now, it will take us like 45 minutes to an hour to get home and I don't think my bladder can wait that long!"

Leah shook her head. "Honestly Jill you should be able to go a couple of hours without a bathroom like that."

"I agree, I can't understand how anyone can depend on public toilets for anything," Patricia said. "I for one would never sit my ass down on a toilet that has been sat upon by dozens of women."

"Well not everybody can go all day without going to the bathroom," Jill said.

"Considering that you enjoy desperation you would think that you would be a little bit better at holding it in," Patricia said. "People are spoiled by the overabundance of public toilets."

"Look I'm willing to do some holding, under controlled circumstances at home when there is a toilet a few feet away without an outrageous wait," Jill said. "It's quite a different matter to have your bladder ready to explode and be in a public place like this, as it's quite embarrassing! And now you are making me shout and people are staring!"

"I'll admit that it is kind of embarrassing to have to use a public toilet altogether," Patricia said.

"Yeah seriously," Leah said. "It doesn't sound very sanitary either, as a lot of these toilets are filthy."

"Oh yeah FYI Jill, the toilets in there are, well let's just say they're not the nicest toilets in the world," Ashley said.

"They're not?" Jill said with a frown. "Wait, you used them!"

"Luckily I know how to hover," Ashley said. "There was no way I was sitting my ass down on one of those nasty ass toilets!"

"I hate it when people hover; they make the toilet nasty for everyone who comes after them!" Jill shouted.

Ashley shook her head. "Well when you see these toilets you will wish that you knew how to hover because I know I certainly wouldn't want to sit down on those. And I was at the front of the line, remember?"

"Yes I very distinctly remember that you got far ahead of me in line!" Jill said.

"But I'm just saying you have a couple of dozen women ahead of you, so I hope that they don't run out of toilet paper," Ashley said. "If I were you I would just wait until I got home."

"Easy for you to say, you got to go to the bathroom already!" Jill shouted as she looked at Henry. "You too, as always."

"It's not my fault that guys can pee a lot easier!" Henry said as he laughed. "I mean I could have easily held it and everything, but you know those sodas."

"Yes I do!" Jill said as she continued dancing in place. "Oh my God I have to go so bad!"

Ashley walked away for a moment and then came back.

"Well you still have about 25 people to go Jill, and that's just outside the bathroom," Ashley said.

"Well okay that's making some progress at least," Jill said as she stepped up. "I'm not even on the stairs anymore!"

"Once again I still think that we should just leave and go home," Ashley said.

"Definitely," Leah said as Patricia nodded in agreement as did Henry.

"But it's your fault I'm in this mess already!" Jill said. "Now we're staying and we're going to wait for me to go to the bathroom and that's final!"

"Says who," Leah said.

"Says my bursting bladder!" Jill said as she crossed her legs tightly and frowned.

"Well you know it is Henry's car," Ashley said. "So technically isn't it his decision?"

"You know I suppose it is," Henry said as he smiled.

"And I'd really like to get home sometime in the next hour," Patricia said. "You know we all have stuff to do to prepare for our first day at work tomorrow."

Leah nodded. "That's a good point; we all really have a busy day tomorrow, so I think that we should get home as quickly as possible."

"I agree, and I think that since Henry was so nice to give us a ride we shouldn't really make him wait," Ashley said.

"Guys like I said my bladder's needs do not respond to a democratic vote!" Jill said.

"You know they kind of have a point, I really shouldn't hold up all these ladies," Henry said. "I think that they really want to go."

"I really want to go!" Jill shouted.

"Okay then let's go," Ashley said as she waved them towards the staircase leading into the lobby.

"You already got to go!" Jill shouted.

"Hey you can't hold that against her that she got to go faster," Henry said.

"Come on let's bail on this place," Ashley said as she waved towards everyone as Henry, Leah and Patricia started walking off with him.

"I think your friends are bailing on you," the woman in line behind Jill said.

"No, they wouldn't do that to me," Jill said as she waved her hands dismissively but watched her friends disappear from sight down the stairs. As she stood there with her legs crossed and saw that her friends weren't coming back suddenly she started getting nervous. She turned to the woman behind her in line. "Do you think you could just hold my space in line for a second?"

"One," the woman said as she laughed. "Okay that was a second. No I'm just joking with you, but I can't promise anything."

Jill quickly got out of line and started walking down the stairs as her friends came back smiling.

"We weren't actually going to leave you Jill," Henry said. "But it looks like it got you out of line!"

Jill quickly started bolting back up the stairs and ran in front of the woman in front of her. "Thanks for holding my place in line for a second," Jill said.

"That second was up a long time ago," the woman said.

"What?" Jill asked.

"No I'm just getting it back in line," the woman said as Jill got in front of her in line.

"Geez Jill, you really thought we were going to leave you here," Ashley said.

"Well generally when people start walking away like that you have to somewhat suspect something is going down," Jill said.

"We wouldn't really leave you Jill, although we really should probably leave," Leah said.

"Don't worry we will stay, but it's only because we find you so damned entertaining," Henry said.

Although Jill couldn't say anything to the other woman in line she knew that it was 100% true, she knew that her friends were having an absolute riot of a time seeing her having to go to the bathroom like that. And again she couldn't blame them, because situation reversed she would have loved to see them in this situation, but that rarely ever happened as it was usually her who was on display for all the world to see.

Fortunately after that the line started moving a little bit faster, and eventually Jill got into the bathroom itself. Finally it was her turn and as she walked into the toilet she had to admit that Ashley was unfortunately 100% right, those weren't the nicest toilet she had ever seen.

"It's times like this I wish I could hover," Jill said as she took a bunch of toilet paper and wiped off the toilet seat before finally sitting down and having a loud hissing pee into the toilet.

As she came out of the toilet a lot more women started entering the restroom and she realized that she had just missed another crowd getting out of the movies. Jill quickly washed her hands and made towards the exit where her friends were waiting.

"45 minutes," Patricia said as she looked at her watch. "We could have been home by now! I hope it was worth it."

"Believe me it was worth it," Jill said as she smiled as she walked with her friends to the car.

"I'm just saying that this is what happens when you rely on public bathrooms too much," Patricia said in the car ride home. "Honestly an adult woman should be able to go out for a few hours without having to reduce herself to using a public toilet like that."

"I don't know how you can possibly hold it all day," Jill said.

"Practice makes perfect, you just give in to your bladder too easily," Patricia said shaking her head. "You really should try holding it longer."

"But again I'm willing to do some holding sometimes, but at home under controlled circumstances, you don't want to take chances with a full bladder when you're out in public and having to interact with people."

"I kind of like the sensation of a full bladder," Patricia said.

"I don't know how you can maintain your composure when your bladder is that full," Jill said. "You probably won't even go to the bathroom all day at work tomorrow."

"Of course I won't, that would be disgusting!"

"Yeah I won't be using the toilets there either," Leah said.

"I'll use them when I get the chance," Ashley said. "But seeing as I have to do all the driving and the deliveries it sometimes is a long stretch between a break."

"Today was payback for all of those times I teased you while you are desperate in your truck wasn't it?" Jill said.

Ashley smiled and nodded. "You bet! I just wish that stuff like this would happen more often."

Jill shook her head. "Well don't get used to it, there is not much that will keep me from a bathroom and situations like this are rare."

Patricia shook her head. "You really should learn not to be a slave to your bladder Jill, a full bladder is a happy bladder after all."

"Only up until the point where it's unbearable!" Jill said. "Some of us may enjoy desperation and holding but at the end of it all we still like to be able to go."

"Well here's my stop," Jill said as the car pulled to a stop and she got out. "I'll see you all tomorrow bright and early at work."

"But not in the bathroom," Patricia said.

"Of course not," Jill said as she closed the car door and shook her head. She was glad that she was finally home, because it was true what they say, once you break the seal you have to go again just soon enough!

2

Jill woke up bright and early the next morning looking forward to her new job. She had not really worked in an office before but she figured the fact that she was going to be working with a lot of her friends would probably make everything fun and interesting. It sounded like an easy enough job where they just had to keep track of the orders and records of people who were buying swimwear and other aquatic gear.

It didn't take long for her friends to arrive to pick her up at the carpool, and luckily it wasn't very far away to the office, which was actually a pretty big complex on a large piece of land. It was a huge place with all sorts of warehouses, files and other inventories. It really was one of the biggest companies as far as selling swimwear and aquatic gear went, so she figured they would probably be busy most of the day.

"Is everybody looking forward to our first new day at our new jobs?" Henry asked.

"Well I have to drive the truck that delivers a lot of these things, so I probably won't get to be spending as much time in the office as you guys," Ashley said. "You should be glad that I got all of you guys' office jobs. I've been working at this company for a while and I have to say that they are the best."

Jill laughed.

"But what is so funny?" Ashley asked.

"Well you said that you were going to be driving the company truck and delivering a lot of the packages, so that probably doesn't give you many opportunities to use the bathroom."

Ashley shook her head. "Honestly sometimes I don't even get to go to the bathroom until lunchtime."

"Jesus I don't know how you go all day without a bathroom like that," Jill said. "We know these two will not be going to the bathroom at all somehow," Jill said as she pointed to Leah and Patricia.

"She's not going all day without a bathroom, she gets to go at lunch, which is more than I think anyone really needs to go to the bathroom," Patricia said. "Honestly who wants to actually use a bathroom at work? People should wait until they get home to go to the bathroom."

"Well an average person has to go to the bathroom at some point during the day," Jill said. "People who can go all day without using the bathroom and maybe just go once a day are rare outliers."

"Well if you had learned to go to the bathroom a little bit less frequently over time your bladder would get stronger and you would have a bladder like mine," Patricia said. "Well maybe not like mine, but bigger than the one you have now."

"To be fair I think that very few people on this earth have a bladder that anywhere approaches yours, but I fully agree with you that you shouldn't have to go to the bathroom during work," Leah said. "It's not that hard to go eight hours without a bathroom."

"Again not for you, but for the average person, the average person goes to the bathroom several times a day," Jill said. "I just hope the bathrooms at this office are immaculate!"

"Jill and her toilets," Ashley said. "I mean we all have an interest in that stuff but you are like George Costanza from Seinfeld, always looking for the perfect toilet everywhere you go. But like I said don't worry, these aren't like those dank ass toilets at the movie theater last night, this is a really swanky and professional place and the toilets are so clean that you can eat off of them."

"I wouldn't even sit on a public toilet, let alone eat off of one," Patricia shouted as she shook her head.

"Well to be fair I never ate my lunch on or off of the toilet," Ashley said. "But the toilets are clean enough for what their intended purposes are, so there is nothing to worry about there."

"Don't take things lightly, you can tell a lot about a place by the condition that they keep their toilets in," Jill said. "A place that provides abundant toilets is a place that cares about their employees and has money to spend."

"They could probably improve efficiency at every company if they just abolished public toilets altogether, so people wouldn't be spending all of their time at the bathroom" Patricia said." But I know Jill's going to say that that's not realistic to have a society without public toilets."

"Of course it's unrealistic to have a society without public toilets, how did we even have society before we had public toilets?" Jill said shaking her head. "When you look at it the history of civilization is the history of plumbing, as civilization was not possible until we had a plumbing system to remove waste."

"I'm not quite as extreme as Patricia, but I do think that probably people shouldn't be spending their time in the toilet while they are at work," Leah said. "But even I don't think that I could function in a world without toilets altogether. But I can easily go throughout the day without subjecting myself to sitting on a toilet at work that all of the other employees have also sat on."

"Hey a toilet doesn't carry the plague, so when you gotta go you gotta go," Jill said.

"I don't feel it's necessarily the case," Patricia said. "Most people go to the bathroom because they want to go to the bathroom, not because they need to go to the bathroom. Most people could put off going to the bathroom a lot more for a longer stretch of time than they usually do. People sometimes want to go as soon as they feel the urge or are the least bit uncomfortable, people need to deal with a little bit more discomfort and not go to the bathroom as soon as possible. It's because of people like you who are always drinking their water everywhere they go and going to the bathroom at their first urge that people never develop sufficient bladder strength in the first place. If you really like desperation you should hold it for a while."

"I can hold it for a while but I'm not going to hold it all day," Jill said. "Not all of us like to hold it to the point where we are in horrible agonizing pain; I mean certainly not when we are at work!"

Patricia put her arm on Jill's shoulder. "If you want to have a bladder capacity like mine you have to play through the pain and have to learn to enjoy the pain."

"Well you can learn to enjoy the pain, but when I am out in public and doing other things I'm going to go to the bathroom before I get uncomfortable, let alone before I am in agonizing gut wrenching pain and keeling over at my desk because my bladder exploded," Jill said.

"Exaggerate much," Henry said as he laughed. "Well looks like we're just about here, ready or not here we come."

The five of them got out of the car and they walked into the office building where they would be working. Jill had to admit as soon as she saw it she thought that the place looked pretty nice, like they had really high standards of efficiency and valued and cared about their employees.

When she walked into the lobby she had to admit that everything was equally nice with lots of potted plants and everything, and even a water fountain in the middle of the room.

"You're right this place is pretty swanky," Henry said as Ashley nodded in agreement. "I mean for a place that basically just processes orders for various swim and aquatic gear and ships them out from the warehouse this is a pretty nice set up."

"I told you it was a really nice company," Ashley said. "I've never really had any complaints about anything and I think the people here are relatively friendly and helpful. You'll see, I think you'll get used to it right away."

They walked down the hallway until they arrived at the office where they were supposed to report and they were shown around.

"Hi I'm Kate," a woman said as she came to greet them and shook all of their hands. "You must be the new employees. As you can see this is a relatively small office but I think that we are a tightknit group. Let me introduce you to the other coworkers that you will be working with." She walked over to a bunch of people all sitting at their computers who looked up and smiled. "Everybody I would like you to meet our new employees Henry, Patricia, Leah and Jill, and I think that you all know Ashley already."

Henry, Patricia, Leah and Jill went around and shook everybody's hand.

"As I already said I am Kate and I am kind of like the supervisor around here, as the most senior employee, but I am looking for somebody to be a vice supervisor and perhaps take on most of my duties, so if you impress me you might get my job one day. But these are your other coworkers Christina, Samantha, Kim, Sarah and Jenny."

"It looks like I'm the only guy in this entire office," Henry said. "But don't worry I assure you I am a perfect gentleman."

"Yes it seems our office is mostly female, so at least no one can accuse us of being sexist," Kate said. "We are a very progressive company who aim to give everybody an equal opportunity. It just seems like most of the people who applied for this office job just happened to be female."

"Women of the world unite," Jill said as several people sort of smiled and laughed.

"Well I guess that I will show you to your desks," Kate said as she sat everyone down in front of computer monitors. "There actually is something that I have been meaning to discuss with you. While all of you are going to be working in this office we do need one person to volunteer for a very special job. It comes with slightly better pay but probably what most people would consider an insignificant amount, like maybe just a few more dollars a day, because it's basically the same job that everybody else has."

"What type of job?" Leah asked.

"It's a job that you are all basically equally qualified for except the location is different," Kate said. "What we need is somebody to operate from the warehouse."

"The warehouse?" Jill asked.

Kate nodded. "The warehouse isn't really connected to the main series of office buildings and is sort of a ways away from the rest of the facilities here. Basically we need somebody to go to the warehouse and check the inventory whenever somebody makes an order. It's also where we keep all of our personal files and everything. So basically what the person who works in the warehouse would be doing was essentially the same as what you would be doing in the office. In fact we will even have you set up at a desk with a computer and you will be in a constant video feed with your fellow coworkers. Basically the person at the warehouse will be the go to girl." Kate looked at Henry. "Or the go to guy, as the case may be."

Jill had to admit that she wanted to stay close to all of her friends but at the same time she looked forward to the idea of possibly slightly higher pay and she wanted to make an impression.

"Are there any downsides to working in the warehouse?" Jill asked.

"Why, are you interested?" Kate said.

"Interested in higher pay I suppose," Jill said. "I mean who wouldn't be?"

"Like I said it's a really insignificant amount but it's an easy enough job," Kate said. "I don't really think that there's any drawback to working in the warehouse, although the accommodations are a bit sparse. The warehouse isn't meant to be as nice-looking as the rest of the office but there's nothing bad about it. The only irritating thing like I said is that it's sort of out-of-the-way, like nearly a half mile away from the main facilities here. It's kind of under construction though as well, so like I said it's not as pretty to look at as the rest of this area."

Jill shrugged her shoulders. "I don't see any drawbacks."

"Does anybody else really want the job?" Kate asked. She looked around and she didn't see anyone jumping at the opportunity, as most of them looked like they were pretty content to be sitting at their office desks in front of a computer all day in the nice office. "Okay Jill I guess you've got the job. Let me just have everybody sign their employee contracts and then we will drive you over to the warehouse and get you set up."

Kate started handing out all the employee contracts and everyone began signing them.

"How come I have an extra contract," Jill said as she flipped to the second page.

"Oh don't worry about that, that's just signing a special thing saying that you don't mind working in the warehouse, as a lot of people would rather not be relegated to the warehouse," Kate said. "You know it's just a minor bureaucratic thing. We said that you would have an office job and technically the warehouse is still in office job but because you are in a different location you just have to sign another additional contract. Again it's nothing but bureaucracy, just sign it and there should be no problem. We pretty much just have to be covered in everything that we do, you know how it is."

"Okay sounds good," Jill said as she finished signing the contract.

"Great," Kate said. "Let me just get the rest of the new workers set up at their stations and then I will escort you down to the warehouse. It's just a little short drive I suppose, no big deal."

"Well Jill I am kind of disappointed that we won't be working in the same office together but I guess we technically are since we will be connected by video chat," Leah said.

"Exactly, it's no different than when we reach out on video elsewhere, we are all people of the Internet age," Jill said. "Although I don't like the way I always look on video camera because I always come out looking like, I don't know, I'm just socially awkward as you know."

"Well hey you're among friends," Patricia said. "It will be fun being able to chat on WebCam all day."

Jill said her goodbyes to her friends as Kate got everybody set up, and then Kate got Jill in the car and started driving her down to the warehouse.

"Why is the warehouse so far away from the rest of the facilities?" Jill asked.

"Well like I said the warehouse is just where we store all of the stuff that we sell, so I'll admit that it's probably going to be a bit lonely with you by yourself most of the day, although people will come through throughout the day in order to pick up orders and ask you to direct them to stuff, but you'll be on video chat with all of your friends throughout the entire day. In fact we have to ask that you keep the video on at all times."

"I don't see a problem with that," Jill said as they continued driving until they arrived at the warehouse. As they approached the warehouse Jill had to admit that it looked lonely and remote. There weren't really any other buildings anywhere in the vicinity and she felt like she had been relegated to the backwoods of the company, but she figured if they were going to pay her slightly more it would be worth it.

They got into the warehouse and Jill saw what looked like rows and rows of inventory just sitting on shelves for as far as the eye could see. It really was a really large warehouse and everything, but it still seemed like a lonely and empty place. She felt like if she shouted that she would hear her echo shouting back at her.

"Here's your desk," Kate said as she sat Jill down at her desk and booted up the computer.

"Jill," Patricia said as her image came on the video monitor.

"Hey," Jill said as she waved and smiled. "Hey the picture resolution on this thing is pretty damn good."

"Only the best at this company," Kate said. "Well okay then I guess now that you're all set up I will get back to the rest of the office workers and you can start your day. Remember if you need anything just ask."

"Thank you," Jill said as she shook Kate's hand and smiled and sat down at her computer station. As she looked around she had to admit that even though she felt really lonely in the warehouse she was connected to her friends to video chat at all times. In fact she could see images of the face of every single employee in the other building and that made her feel less lonely, but also kind of like she was being watched, cause technically she was.

It didn't take long for lots of orders to come in, and every time a new order came in Jill would have to diligently get up and check the inventory to make sure that they had it. She had to admit that it was a lot of walking and she was kind of expecting to be sitting at a desk all day, but she figured that since she was mostly still sitting at her desk it probably suited her lazy lifestyle.

One of the things that Jill didn't like about the warehouse however was that it was kind of hot and stuffy, especially around now in the beginning of summer. As a result of that she found herself getting thirsty rather quickly and found herself drinking more than she normally would.

Finally at around two hours into work Jill first started to notice that she had to go to the bathroom. Unfortunately the orders were just pouring in so she didn't really have time to stop and take a break. Finally after about 2 1/2 hours there was a slow stretch where not much was happening.

"Okay time for a bathroom break," Jill said as she got up from her station and began looking around. That was when she noticed something. As she looked around the warehouse all she saw were rows and rows of inventory. The whole place was extremely large but Jill figured that the bathroom should be located nearby. However as she got up and started looking around she noticed something very unusual. "Where the hell is the freaking bathroom?" Jill said realizing that she had looked up and down the place and figured that she just missed it somewhere.

Finally she came back to her desk.

"Jill, where were you?" Patricia asked.

"I was doing something that you never do, I was looking for the damn bathroom," Jill said.

"Well you were gone an awful long time and we were wondering where you went," Patricia said. "But now that you're back from the bathroom we have a couple of new orders for you to see if we have them in stock."

"No that's just the thing though; I didn't go to the bathroom!"

"What do you mean you didn't go to the bathroom, you said that you were just looking for the bathroom."

"Yes I said I was looking for the bathroom, not that I found the bathroom."

"What's the matter," Kate said as her face came onto the screen. "Where you have you been Jill, we have been looking for you?"

"Kate I have to ask you something," Jill said now getting a little bit antsy.

"What is it?" Kate said.

"I can't believe I didn't ask you when I first got here as usually it's the thing that I ask about right away, but where exactly is the ladies room in this building?"

"What do you mean?"

"I mean where's the damn bathroom?! I looked up and down and I think that I looked over the entire place but I just couldn't find the damn thing."

Kate laughed. "Oh, well there's a simple reason for that."

"What's that?"

Kate laughed again. "Because there is no bathroom in the warehouse."

3

"What do you mean there is no bathroom in the warehouse?!" Jill shouted.

"Just what I said, there's no bathroom in the warehouse," Kate said shrugging her shoulders. "Why is that so hard to understand?"

"How do you not have a bathroom in the warehouse?"

"Well as was explained in the contract that you signed when you agreed to work the warehouse job is that the warehouse was very sparse and was mostly just a bunch of inventory. The fact is the whole place has been under construction, and since nobody really inhabited the warehouse we didn't really find it necessary to install a bathroom. We figured that the cost would be prohibitive and it was just simply not necessary and there's also really no place in the warehouse to put a bathroom. I mean look around you, where do you think it would fit?"

"Once again I ask you, how do you not have a bathroom in every building?"

Kate shrugged her shoulders. "Like I said, I guess they just never saw fit to install one in the warehouse. Have I answered all of your questions?"

"You most certainly did not! I mean what if I supposed to do if I have to –" Jill said suddenly blushing.

"But if you have to what?" Kate asked and Jill thought that she distinctly saw a little bit of a smirk on her face.

"But what if I have to go to the bathroom," Jill whispered.

"What was that?" Kate asked.

"I said what if I have to go to the freaking bathroom?!" Jill shouted causing all of her coworkers to take notice.

"Well I suppose you could go to your bathroom during your break, except you already used up your break for the next two hours," Kate said as she looked at her watch.

"I can't really use the bathroom during my break if there is no bathroom, now can I?"

"The nearest bathroom is here in the office building where all of your coworkers are."

"That's a half mile away, how am I supposed to go a half mile and then another half mile back during a 15 minute break?"

Kate scratched her head. "You know I hadn't really thought about that."

"How could you not have thought about it?"

Kate shrugged her shoulders. "I guess the issue has just never come up before."

"But how does this not be an issue?"

"I don't know, the last guy didn't seem to have a problem when he was assigned to the warehouse."

That was when all of the sudden it hit Jill. She was probably the first woman to be working in the warehouse department. She figured the first people before her were probably all guys and they probably just went and peed in the parking lot or something like that. In fact just at that moment she noticed in the corner was what looked like a small can that didn't look very sanitary.

"Maybe you could send that little cart that you drove me here in," Jill said.

"The transport vehicle is not there to ferry employees back and forth from the bathroom. It's pretty much in constant use throughout the day. Once you get dropped off it's pretty much being used all day to transport things around the facilities. We simply cannot spare it Jill."

"What am I supposed to do if I need the bathroom?"

Kate once again shook her head and shrugged her shoulders. "I guess you'll just have to hold it in."

"That sounds like it's simple enough," Patricia said as Leah nodded in agreement.

"Well anyway I think that you all better be getting back to work, I'm not paying you to idle around," Kate said as she disappeared.

"Wait," Jill said that Kate had already vanished.

"You hold Kate, I mean you heard Kate, we have to get back to work Jill," Leah said.

"Yeah Jill, this is exactly why we told you that you shouldn't always rely so much on public toilets," Patricia said. "Now we have another order coming up that we need you to check."

Jill wanted to argue with them but she realized that it was kind of futile, so as the order came in she started getting up and checking the inventory. As she walked over to look at the inventory she had to admit that the walking was making her have to go to the bathroom more, but she figured if she just put it out of her head maybe she could ignore the urge as Patricia and Leah did all day.

Eventually Jill came back with the order and reported back to her coworkers. She had to admit though that now she was starting to notice that she had to go to the bathroom distinctly more. She couldn't believe that the urge took so long to hit her, but now she couldn't really ignore it.

While Jill got a moment of downtime she looked at the time and realized that she still had three more hours until work was over, and she was already getting uncomfortable. She soon found herself watching the clock almost obsessively, like a prisoner on death row awaiting their final hour. However her job kept her relatively busy, so she didn't have that much time to sit there and contemplate her bladder, even though she certainly couldn't ignore it either.

Luckily soon it was lunchtime, so she had at least a half hour now, but she knew that it was still impossible to get to a bathroom in time. It was just not realistic for her to run all the way to the other office building and all the way back. She figured that it would probably take her at least an hour. She thought maybe her friends could drive her over but they didn't allow any vehicles other than the transport cart to go over to the warehouse, for some ridiculous reason. Plus her friends were supposed to stay on call even during lunch. Because they had a relatively short workday they were expected to eat their lunch while doing their jobs.

Fortunately however there was a little bit of downtime. So while Jill's coworkers were busy starting to eat their lunch she started looking around the warehouse. Once again she looked at the small can in the corner and shook her head.

"No way am I peeing into that bacteria trap," Jill said as she decided to maybe go get some fresh air because it was rather stuffy in the warehouse. As she walked out into the open air she had to admit she felt a little bit better but also had to admit that the pressure in her bladder was growing in a way that she couldn't ignore.

Jill started looking around and saw that nobody seemed to be coming. Did she dare attempt to pop a squat? She had never peed outside before but she was strongly feeling the urge to maybe try. She didn't think she could do it without peeing all over herself though, she had no balance and she was definitely not the outdoors type in general, which is precisely why she decided to take an office job in the first place.

Jill continued to pace around the warehouse and she knew that she was fiddling with her skirt, which was a nervous habit that she had when she knew she had to go to the bathroom. It's like she almost instinctively wanted to jerk it down and have a pee.

As Jill was contemplating what she could do about her increasingly filling by the minute bladder, she noticed that there seemed to be cameras mounted on poles all around the warehouse. She shook her head and realized that whatever she might have been thinking of doing before she certainly wasn't going to do now.

"Big brother maybe watching us but I'm not going to let him watch me pop a squat in the parking lot and pee all over myself!" Jill said as someone went by and she waved discreetly. Now however she could barely ignore the fact that she had to go to the bathroom but figured she had better get back to the warehouse.

She sat down back at her desk to see that Patricia was drinking quite a bit. Seeing her drinking made Jill kind of thirsty, and even though she knew it was probably not wise, she started drinking more of her drink that she had brought for lunch. She only took small sips because she knew that apple juice tended to make her have to go to the bathroom even more, and she certainly didn't need that right now.

"This place is pretty nice," Leah finally said on the video monitor.

"Yeah I totally agree, this is one of the nicest offices I have ever worked in," Patricia said as she continued to drink her drink. "What you think about it Jill?"

"I am in a stuffy warehouse that doesn't have a bathroom," Jill said shaking her head.

"Once again you have to go back to this fixation with bathrooms," Patricia said.

"It's not a fixation, places should have bathrooms!" Jill shouted. "You guys all have a bathroom."

"Like I would actually use it," Patricia said as she gave a look of disgust to which Leah gave a similar look as she nodded in agreement.

"At least you have the option to use it if you really needed it," Jill said.

"What's going on," Henry said as he came out of the door of the office bathroom.

"I have to go to the bathroom!" Jill said, once again practically shouting.

"So what's the problem, go to the bathroom," Henry said.

"There is no bathroom in the warehouse!" Jill shouted.

"So what do you do if you have to pee?" Henry said trying to suppress an obvious smile.

"Exactly!" Jill shouted. "This is entirely unfair, how can they give you guys a bathroom right there in the office with you and give me nothing?"

"Well you did kind of agree to work in the warehouse," Leah said. "So I guess you really can't complain."

"Of course I can complain!" Jill shouted. "I can complain a whole lot. Is it really so outrageous that I took that job in the assumption that, I don't know, I would be able to go to the bathroom at some point during the day?"

Patricia shook her head. "Once again I don't understand why they have public bathrooms at all."

"Because most of us need a bathroom at some point during the day, and I definitely do need one right now," Jill said.

"So why don't you go to the bathroom?" Henry said. "I don't see what the big deal is."

"You mean go to the bathroom outside like some animal?" Jill said shaking her head. "No thank you. Besides in case you didn't notice all of the security cameras everywhere, they're watching our every move."

Patricia nodded. "Now there's a sensible thing, people shouldn't be such slaves to their bladders that they have to go to the bathroom outdoors squatting like some type of animal with no self-control."

"I have a lot of self-control, and I am using every last bit of it right now," Jill said as everyone noticed that she was now crossing her legs.

"Jill you should just learn to control yourself," Patricia said. "I feel like this is your wake-up call from the universe. It's telling you that you're a grown up now and that you should be able to get through the day without having to visit the bathroom every five minutes."

"But it hasn't been five minutes, it has been three or 3 1/2 hours!" Jill shouted and people could now see that she was shaking her leg a little bit.

"Well look at the bright side, only 2 1/2 hours left to go before the end of the day," Leah said.

"Only 2 1/2 hours!" Jill shouted. "You know very well that that's an eternity when you have to pee."

"I don't have a problem getting through the entire day without a bathroom, so you shouldn't either," Leah said as Patricia sat there smiling and nodding and giving a thumbs-up.

"Well not all of us have the bladders of an Amazon warrior," Jill said. "Some of us need to go to the bathroom throughout the day, and I really really need the bathroom right now."

"But you should probably just try not to think about it then," Henry said.

Jill started tapping her foot nervously in her seat. "How can I not think about going to the bathroom when I work at a place that sells swimwear and aquatic gear? Basically everything that we are talking about all day is water this and water that, liquid this and liquid that."

Henry laughed. "You know I didn't even really think about that all that much, I guess I never really contemplated the irony of the fact that we have an interest in pee and we are working at a place that essentially is selling all sorts of water sports related equipment, you know a different sort of water sports though."

"Yeah I'd rather not think about that right now," Jill said as she crossed and uncrossed her legs.

"Well then just think about focusing on your job, because that's what we are here to do," Patricia said. "Our lunch break is almost over, so we're going to have to be getting back to work pretty soon."

Once again Jill wanted to protest, but she realized that lunch hour was over and that she would have to find some way to deal with the situation and get through the next 2 1/2 hour somehow. Of course as she looked at the clock every five minutes to see it moving at a painstakingly slow pace she was getting more and more impatient.

By the time they had reached the four hour mark Jill had to admit she was frantic. She couldn't help but cross and uncross her legs and shift around in her seat.

"Hey Jill is something bothering you, you look overly antsy, like you've got ants in your pants or something," Samantha said. "Anyway I've got another order for you."

Jill very slowly got up from her seat and she could feel all of the pressure rushing into her bladder which caused her to bend at the knees a little bit as she very slowly walked over to the inventory area. She barely even noticed the fact that she was crossing her ankle over her other ankle and doing little squats while she was looking for the inventory, but Leah, Patricia and Henry were certainly noticing, and they were watching her every movement with great interest.

"Here, I got the file," Jill said as she sat back down very slowly at her computer and once again sort of started sitting leaning sideways with her legs crossed and then her ankles crossed over each other.

"Good work Jill," Samantha said as Jill reviewed the file and gave her the necessary information about the product at hand. Samantha then started looking towards the back of the room.

"Are you looking for something?" Jill said as she crossed and uncrossed her legs and began shaking one of her legs a little bit.

Samantha laughed. "Oh it's nothing, it's just seeing you sort of squirming around like that, it kind of made me realize I have to go to the bathroom, so I will be right back. Don't go anywhere Jill."

"Where exactly would I go?" Jill said. And as she said the word go she kept thinking of that particular meaning of go, as in go to the bathroom. She knew that she would really really really like to go at the moment, and the fact that Samantha was getting to practically made her want to scream.

"Thanks Jill, I'll just be gone a minute," Samantha said.

"Sure take your time, no need to rush on my account," Jill said as she gritted her teeth.

"How are you holding up Jill?" Patricia said with a big smile on her face.

"Well I'm holding, I know that much," Jill said as she impatiently tapped her feet on the floor and began shaking her legs again.

Patricia smiled even wider. "That's good Jill, that's very very good. But you should try to be a little bit more professional, do you really have to be shaking your legs and tapping your feet like that."

"Do you think I would be doing so if I didn't really very badly have to," Jill said as she tried to control her shaking to some degree.

"I'm back," Samantha said with a huge look of relief on her face and a big beaming smile. "Sorry I kept you so long Jill, but I really had to go, you know how it is."

"Yeah I kind of do," Jill said trying to suppress her legs from shaking and to remain as composed and calm and collected as possible.

"Oh wait, sorry I forgot Jill," Samantha said as she laughed before controlling herself. "Sorry I didn't mean to laugh."

"No of course you didn't, I mean it's so hilarious that your coworker doesn't have a bathroom all day long," Jill said trying not to be angry and rude but finding it harder to compose herself by the moment.

"Well I think we have another order coming in, so you know what to do," Samantha said still looking smiling and very chipper.

Jill got up from her seat very slowly and sort of waddled over to the inventory to see if they had the particular product that Samantha was looking for, and she walked over very slowly, pausing every few minutes and bending at the knees, before she brought it back to the computer.

"Is this the one we needed?" Jill said as he put what looked like a scuba mask down on the table and held it up to the computer monitor.

"That is a blue mask, I think the person said that they wanted an orange one," Samantha said. "Would you mind getting up and looking for the orange one?"

"But of course, it's my job isn't it," Jill said gritting her teeth and trying not to be angry but finding it very hard to disguise the agitation in her voice.

Very slowly Jill once again waddled over to the inventory, stood there with her legs tightly crossed and visible to everyone on the computer monitor, and had to suppress the urge to stick her hands between her legs and grab herself because she knew that that would be very a very unprofessional thing to do on the job.

"Okay here's the orange scuba mask," Jill said as she held it up and slowly sat down once again crossing and uncrossing her legs really tightly, like they were the jaws of life or something.

The next hour passed painstakingly slow. All of Jill's

coworkers seemed like they were happy and cheerful, and several of them went to the bathroom during that time, but not Patricia or Leah of course, Jill knew that she would never see that happen at work, even if they were trapped there in a hostage siege situation for 12 hours straight and were taken prisoner.

Finally the day was almost over and Jill could barely sit still in her seat. She had to admit that she was blushing and anxious because she knew that it was perfectly obvious, even to people who didn't have a pee desperation fetish, that she had to go, and that she had to go very very badly.

"Okay everybody, that's it for today," Kate finally said and Jill practically wanted to cry tears of joy that the day was finally over. "We will send the cart over to pick you up Jill. It might take us a couple of minutes; I hope you don't mind waiting?"

"No, of course not, why would I mind waiting," Jill said sucking in air through her teeth and trying to maintain her composure without looking like a vein was about to burst in her forehead.

"We will be waiting for you Jill, to drive home," Patricia said.

As Jill sat there looking at the computer monitor she couldn't help but notice several of her other coworkers used the bathroom before the day was over. At that moment all she could think about was getting relief. She couldn't remember the last time she had to pee so bad and she was about ready to scream.

Finally the cart arrived to pick Jill up.

"So how was your first day?" Kate asked.

"Oh it was wonderful, this is a wonderful place," Jill said trying not to sound sarcastic but failing miserably. She also couldn't suppress the fact that she was now rapidly crossing and uncrossing her legs and tapping her feet in the back of the cart.

When they finally arrived back at the office building Jill practically jumped up out of the cart, but as soon as she stood up she could feel all of the pressure once again cascading to her bladder and she practically was whimpering.

"Have a nice night," Kate said.

"Don't worry we will," Jill said as she waved to Kate before turning back to Henry, Ashley, Leah and Patricia as she stood there with her legs scissored together bobbing up and down and practically in tears.

Ashley looked at the others before looking at Jill and smiling very evilly realizing what had happened, Jill figuring that her friends already told her what the situation was. "So Jill how was the first day?"

"Let me just use the bathroom before we leave," Jill said as she walked over to the door of the office building to find it locked.

"I forgot to tell you that they close down the buildings right away at the end of the day," Patricia said. "But don't worry; we will be home soon enough." That was when she noticed that Jill was practically trembling in place and looked like she was about to faint. "Are you okay Jill?"

Jill quickly ran to the car and looked at Henry. "Drive, drive now like it was the end of the world and your life depended on it!"

4

"Wow Jill, you look like you are in some kind of a rush or something," Henry said as he laughed.

"Get the car in motion right now!" Jill shouted as she bawled her hands into fists and danced in place.

"Say pretty please," Henry said as he held up his keys.

"Car, now!" Jill growled as she stood there crossing and uncrossing her legs. "Pretty please open the damn car right now before I scream at the top of my lungs!"

Henry shrugged his shoulders and started putting the key in the door. "Okay then, whatever you say."

Everyone piled into the car as Jill sat down very slowly on the seat.

"God Jill you really are a drama Queen, you couldn't possibly need the bathroom that badly," Patricia said.

"Totally not in the mood for this right now," Jill said as she sat there with her legs crossed shaking her leg.

"Damn Jill you're about to measure on the Richter scale with all that leg shaking that you are doing," Leah said.

"Just get me home and to a bathroom as fast as possible!" Jill said as she grabbed herself.

"I thought we were all going to go out for drinks to celebrate our first day of work," Ashley said.

"I'm up for that," Leah said as everyone else started nodding in agreement.

"I need a bathroom!" Jill shouted. "I don't think that I've ever needed a bathroom so badly in my entire life."

"You seem like you need a bathroom every couple of minutes," Patricia said. "Is it really that hard to hold it once in a while?"

"Yes!" Jill shouted as she tightly gripped the seat.

"Well the bar is actually closer than your house Jill," Ashley said. "And don't worry you know they have bathrooms."

"Yeah, bathrooms with really long lines," Jill said as she continued tapping her feet furiously.

"Well I already got off on the road to go to the bar," Henry said. "Hopefully there won't be a long line, although it always is fun watching you dance around in line, you are one of the best pee dancers around."

"Not funny guys," Jill said as she struggled to concentrate on something other than the immense pressure in her bladder.

"Situation reversed you know that you would find this hilarious," Ashley said.

"Guys this isn't any ordinary pee, it's a I haven't gone to the freaking bathroom all freaking day type of pee," Jill said.

"That's pretty much every pee for me," Patricia said. "It's always really satisfying to pee at the end of the day after holding it all day. Like the saying goes, good things come to those who wait."

"Not always, sometimes it's a soaked toilet seat that comes to those that wait," Ashley said as she laughed. "God Jill you are too entertaining."

"Get me to a bathroom right now!" Jill shouted.

"Well I'm not going to get a speeding ticket Jill," Henry said.

"I need a bathroom!" Jill said as she kicked the back of Henry's seat.

"Okay I guess I could speed up a little while still staying within the speed limit," Henry said as he started to drive a little faster as all the sudden they hit a speed bump.

"Oh my God, watch the speed bumps!" Jill shouted as she began breathing heavily.

"First you want me to go faster and now you want me to slow down to avoid the speed bumps, which is it," Henry said.

"Whatever is going to get me to the bathroom fastest!" Jill shouted. "Just hurry up!"

Henry started going a little bit faster and Jill screamed every time they hit a speed bump, but eventually they arrived at the bar. Everybody piled out of the car as Jill walked out very slowly and approached the door.

"Gangway I have to pee!" Jill said as she pushed open the door and quickly started running towards the back of the bar where the bathrooms were. As usual there was a line at the ladies room with at least three women in front of her. She tapped the woman in front of her in line.

"Yes?" the woman said as she turned around looking annoyed.

"Normally I would never ask this because it's really awkward, but do you think maybe I can cut you in line for the bathroom?"

"Umm no, sorry."

"Why not?!" Jill said as she stood there dancing in place.

"Because I got here first, why should I let you go ahead of me?"

"Like I said I normally wouldn't ask this but this is like a super bathroom emergency, I haven't gone to the bathroom all day long."

"That's not my fault, you should have gone sooner."

"Well I would have liked to go sooner but I just didn't have the chance all day because my god damn job didn't put a bathroom in the warehouse and, well it's a really long story, but let's just say I really really need that bathroom really bad."

"Well I guess that's too bad then isn't it, it's not my problem," the woman said as she turned back around.

"Please just try to hurry up!"

"Maybe I will, maybe I won't," the woman said as she

smirked. "It's a free country, I can take as long as I like."

"Show some consideration for your fellow citizens."

Jill stood there with her legs tightly crossed bobbing up and down with her hands on her knees slapping herself on the knees breathing heavily.

Meanwhile Jill's friends were waiting at the front of the bar where they could see Jill squirming and dancing.

"Jill really needs to learn some more self-control," Patricia said as Leah nodded in agreement.

"Although I have to admit I can't believe that she managed to go the entire day without a bathroom," Leah said. "That was something I would never think that I would ever live to see, and I have to say it was rather satisfying."

"I'll say," Ashley said. "I wish I was in the office with all of you guys watching Jill squirm all day. I mean it is satisfying knowing that she had to wait all day, but you guys are getting a free show while I was out driving the truck and delivering all the packages."

"Do you think we should go see how Jill is doing," Henry asked.

"Well I think that you know how much Jill hates to be bothered while she is waiting in line for the bathroom and about to explode," Ashley said as she smiled. "So yeah, let's go see how she's doing."

The four of them walked over to where Jill was now second in line.

"I told you guys there would be a line!" Jill shouted. "You know there's always a line of places like this."

Leah shook her head. "You should just be glad that the line isn't longer."

"When I have to go this badly every minute is like an hour," Jill said as she bit down on her lip.

"Don't worry you're next in line, it's not the end of the world," Patricia said.

"Easy for you to say when you have a bladder the size of an Olympic swimming pool!" Jill shouted.

The four of them stood there with her as Jill stood in front of the door dancing in place. Eventually Jill started whistling before she started pounding on the door.

"What's going on in there, you've been in there for a good 10 minutes!" Jill shouted as by now three more people were behind her in line.

"Wait your turn, I will be out in a minute!" the woman shouted as Jill heard the toilet flush and the sound of running water.

"Hurry up!" Jill said. "What time is it? I feel like I have been here for an hour."

Leah looked at her watch. "It's almost 6 PM. Wait, it's Monday isn't it?"

"Yeah, why?" Jill asked.

"Hey you are right, isn't this that bar that does that thing on Mondays at around this time," Ashley said. "What was that thing?"

"Ladies and gentlemen welcome to the Monday night bladder buster!" the bartender announced on a microphone. "You know the rules, everybody drinks free until the first person uses the bathroom or leaves the bar."

"Wow that was satisfying," the woman said as she came out of the ladies room smirking at Jill.

Jill was about to bolt into the bathroom but that was when one of the security guards came and closed the door and shook his head.

"No please, I just need to use the bathroom really quick and then you can begin the bladder buster," Jill said.

"It looks like some people want to end the bladder buster before it even begins," the bartender said. "If you don't want to be the ones to end the bladder buster I would get away from that bathroom door ladies."

"No, this is a nightmare, this can't be happening!" Jill shouted as she stood there with her legs tightly crossed bobbing up and down.

"I guess we should have gotten here faster," Henry said as he laughed. "But hey, free drinks, who's up for it?"

Everyone else in their group started nodding in agreement and started walking away.

"Come on Jill, you don't want to be the one to ruins

everyone's fun, do you?" Ashley said.

"This isn't fun," Jill said as she started walking towards the bathroom door before Ashley grabbed her by the hand and pulled her over to the corner.

"What are you doing?" Jill asked, still practically shaking in place.

Ashley pointed to all the people in the bar staring in their general direction. "I don't think you want to make all these people really angry now do you Jill?"

"No," Jill said. "But I really really need the bathroom."

"I really don't think you want to do that Jill," Ashley said as she once again pointed to all of the people glaring angrily in her direction.

"Dammit!" Jill said practically in tears as Ashley slowly led her over to the bar area where she very slowly and carefully sat down on a barstool.

"Maybe you should have a drink, maybe that would calm you down," Patricia said.

Jill shook her head.

Patricia shook her head right back. "Honestly Jill this is exactly what I was saying again, your obsession with always getting to the nearest public restroom is always causing you trouble."

"Bladder buster," Jill said shaking her head. "This is the most ridiculous idea in the world and it's discriminatory against people with smaller bladders. Who thought of this crazy idea?!"

"I think it's kind of a good idea, it encourages people to hold it and show some discipline and then rewards them for it," Patricia said.

Leah nodded. "Yeah I love bladder buster, it's a whole lot of fun."

"I'm not having a lot of fun right now," Jill said as she sat there in the barstool with her legs tightly crossed. "I'm going out of my mind."

"Mind over bladder Jill, like you are always saying, desperation is 90% psychological," Leah said.

"Not when your bladder is this full," Jill said as she pounded her fists on the counter of the bar.

"Yeah Jill but you certainly don't want to be the one to end the bladder buster," Ashley said. "But hey look at the bright side, with all the drinking that people are doing here their bladders will fill up in no time flat. I'm sure you won't have to wait very long. Just think of all these people in the bar with their bladders slowly filling up, the warm urine pooling around in their bladders pressing against their bladder walls ready to burst like the Hoover dam!"

"Shut up!" Jill shouted as she furiously shook her legs around.

"Sorry Jill, it's just it so much fun to torture you when you are like this," Ashley said. "Honestly this is one of the best nights ever."

"Guys I don't think I can handle this job," Jill said as she bounced in her seat.

"Nonsense, I thought you did a great job today," Patricia said.

"Yeah Jill you were really on top of your game," Leah said. "I think this is a job that is really well-suited to you."

"Not without a bathroom it isn't!" Jill shouted. "To me the ideal job is a job where there are abundant bathrooms for everyone."

"Well no job is perfect Jill," Patricia said.

"I'm not asking for a job to be some type of perfect utopia, but I think a very basic requirement of any job is that they have bathrooms!" Jill shouted as she shook her head. "Don't you think it's unfair that you all have access to a bathroom all day whenever you want and I don't, and I have to interact with you on videoconference the entire time?"

Patricia shook her head. "No Jill, I don't think it's unfair at all."

"Why on earth not, how is that not the most unfair thing in the world?!"

"Well I hardly think that not having a bathroom 5 feet away every second is quite as bad as children dying of leukemia or natural disasters or anything like that."

Everyone nodded in agreement with Patricia.

"Okay so maybe it's not the worst thing in the world, so I exaggerated a little, but it is still pretty terrible. I mean what type of job doesn't have a bathroom?"

"Your job Jill," Leah said as she laughed.

"It's not funny," Jill said.

"Oh bullshit, if it were someone else you knew who was stuck in the warehouse you'd be laughing your ass off just like everyone else," Ashley said. "Need I remind you that you always felt it was kind of funny that I didn't have a bathroom while I was delivering the packages for hours on end? You know I don't get very frequent bathroom breaks either some days."

"Infrequent bathroom breaks some of the time is different than no bathroom breaks whatsoever all of the time," Jill said shaking her head. "You may not get to go to the bathroom for a long time but you eventually do get to go to the bathroom at some point during the day. I don't get to go to the bathroom at all. I can't even go to the bathroom during lunch or immediately after work. I have been sentenced to some type of bathroom purgatory where I must burn off the sins of my enjoyment of desperation before I can enter the Paradise of abundant toilets for everyone."

"Okay now you are just getting theological about it, which is kind of ridiculous," Leah said. "It was just a stressful first day, but I'm sure that once you get used to it that it will be fine."

"I don't want to get used to it! I want them to give me a damn bathroom. How am I supposed to work under these conditions?"

"Well you could always go pee in that can," Henry said. "I mean that's what I would do if I really had to go to the bathroom bad enough."

"Easy for you to say, you have a penis!" Jill shouted as people started looking at her so she got quiet. "But that's probably what happened, all of the people before me who had this job were guys and they probably just peed in that can, that can which is a bacteria trap."

"Well you could always go outside and maybe pee in the parking lot or something like that," Henry said.

Jill shook her head again. "Nope they have surveillance cameras all over the place in the parking lot. Aside from the fact that I can't really squat without peeing all over myself and exposing myself, there is no way I am going to pee in front of surveillance cameras."

"Big brother is watching you pee," Leah said. "I always knew that he probably had a soft spot for water sports."

"Somehow I doubt this is what Orwell had in mind," Jill said as she shook her head. "Seriously guys I really don't have any options. I'm pretty much on camera the entire day, so anything that I do people are going to see. I'm not going to pee in some type of bacteria filled coffee can, and I'm not going to go outside and pee in front of the surveillance cameras, squatting like some animal."

"Well I agree with you on that for sure," Patricia said. "People shouldn't go outside squatting like animals unless it's a real emergency. A real lady holds it."

"When my bladder is this full I am no lady, I'm a total bitch," Jill said as everybody laughed. "I don't know what I'm going to do. And for Christ's sake I really need to go to the bathroom and I need to go to the bathroom now!"

"Don't do it Jill," Ashley said as she pushed Jill back down on her barstool. "But I think I might have found some way out of your predicament if you want to hear it."

Jill nodded. "Yes I want to hear it, please tell me, I would do anything to get out of this predicament, or this peedicament as the case may be."

"Oh so now you want my help and advice and counsel," Ashley said. "You didn't seem to be trying to help me when I was stuck in the truck and we were communicating on phone and you thought it was funny that I had no bathroom around while you were going to the bathroom. Why should I help you right now?"

"Please Ashley, we are friends aren't we?"

Ashley stroked her chin. "Well I suppose I could help you out. First I want you to say please goddess Ashley, please forgive me for making fun of you when your bladder was in distress."

"No way am I saying that," Jill said as she sat there with her hand between her legs.

Ashley shrugged her shoulders. "Well okay if you don't want my advice, I guess we'll figure something out."

As Ashley began whistling Jill continued shaking her leg and squirming in her seat before looking at Ashley. "Please goddess

Ashley, please forgive me for making fun of you when your bladder was in distress."

Ashley sort of shook her head and waved her hand in a dismissive manner. "I don't know, I didn't quite believe that, I feel like you're only saying that because you need my help right now."

Jill continued to tremble in her seat before she gritted her teeth and reluctantly looked at Ashley. "Please my good friend goddess Ashley, who has been so good to me who is so undeserving of your advice and counsel, I humbly submit myself before you and ask you for advice on how to get out of my terrible predicament before my bladder explodes."

"What do you think guys?" Ashley asked.

"I don't know, I think that maybe Jill should drink a little before you give her any advice," Leah said. "Remember, it's free after all."

"Under the circumstances I don't think that would be the wisest thing to be doing right now," Jill said.

"Then maybe it's not the wisest thing for me to advise you," Ashley said.

Jill grabbed a nearby glass and began chugging it down before slamming it down on the table. "There I drank; now please please please tell me how I can get out of this nightmare situation."

Ashley pointed to a bunch of girls over in the corner not far away from the bathroom looking mighty unhappy. "See those girls over there?" Ashley said.

Jill nodded. "Hey, those are the three girls behind me in line for the bathroom."

Ashley nodded and smiled. "Exactly, you're not the only girl here who has to pee really badly. Those girls didn't get to use the bathroom before the bladder buster began either, so they are probably in the same situation as you. Look you can even see some of them crossing their legs."

"Hey you're right," Jill said. "Odds are they won't be able to last much longer, so now all that I have to do is wait for one of them to use the bathroom and I am off the hook."

"And in the meantime we will have fun watching them squirm," Henry said as everybody laughed and nodded.

"Easy for you guys to say, when I have to go this badly it's just a reminder of my own situation," Jill said. "That said they do look rather cute squirming around, don't they?"

Everyone started nodding and saying things like mhhhmmm and licking their lips as they continued drinking.

After about 10 or 15 minutes of watching them however it didn't look likely that they were going to go to the bathroom. A couple of the girls were pacing around and looking anxious but none of them were making a beeline for the bathroom.

"Why aren't any of them going to the bathroom?" Jill said as she continued grabbing herself and crossing her legs.

"For the same reason that you aren't, you don't want to be the one to end everybody's free drinks," Henry said. "Maybe you should go over and talk to them."

"And say what?" Jill asked as she paced back and forth stopping every few seconds to cross her legs and grab herself.

Henry shrugged his shoulders. "I don't know, but if I were you I would try to get them to go to the bathroom as quickly as possible."

Jill shrugged her shoulders and very slowly tiptoed to where the other three girls behind her in line were. There was a blonde girl, an Asian girl and a black girl, all of whom looked decidedly uncomfortable and a bit shifty in the leg area.

"How's it going," Jill said not sure exactly what to say under the circumstances. They all sort of nodded and smiled politely without saying much. "So this bladder buster, pretty stupid idea isn't it?"

The three of them nodded at Jill as they stood there looking at each other. They continued looking at each other as they crossed and uncrossed their legs. They looked over and Jill could see her friends looking over and smiling.

"So –" Jill began saying but not having the slightest idea of what to say in the circumstance.

"You're hoping that one of us is going to go to the bathroom before you aren't you," the black girl said.

"But that's not going to happen," the Asian woman said.

"Yeah, we have experience with this," the blonde girl said.

"So if you're going to be waiting for us to use the bathroom I think you'll be waiting quite some time."

"Okay then, I guess we will wait," Jill said as the four of them started standing there all very obviously crossing their legs and squirming around in place, staring at each other, and they could see that everybody else in the bar was staring at them as well.

Several minutes passed and Jill could feel her bladder screaming out for relief, and she knew that she didn't have much time. She looked at the three girls with her and saw that they were all clearly frantic, but none of them was willing to make the first move. A couple of them started whistling as they stood there in place crossing and uncrossing their legs.

The three girls looked at each other and then they looked at Jill and Jill looked back at them. They knew that it was some type of crazy ass female desperation version of a Mexican standoff and it was only a matter of time before one of them blinked.

Jill's leg was shaking like crazy, and although she didn't want to show weakness, she could see that the other three girls were smiling, because they could tell that she was reaching the breaking point. As Jill stood there shaking and jogging in place she began to become self-conscious as she could see everybody in the bar watching her. Finally the three girls around her started making lots of hissing noises.

Jill felt her legs shaking like she was about to fall down on the floor. She knew that she wasn't going to win this thing, and she certainly wasn't going to have an accident in front of an entire audience like that. She very slowly and subtly started making her way towards the bathroom but the bouncer at the door shook his head.

Jill continued to stand there feeling like an idiot with these other three girls hoping that one of them would blink before she did. But she knew it was futile, even if she was going to end up being the most hated person in the bar she knew what she had to do.

"I'm sorry I have to pee!" Jill said as she pushed open the bathroom door, jerked down her skirt and began peeing furiously as she moaned with relief, practically screaming as she felt her eyes filling with tears. After washing her hands she reluctantly reached for the door knob knowing that when she did she was going to meet an angry mob howling for her blood the second she got out of the bathroom. She thought it was amazing how one simple thing like free drinks could turn people against their fellow human beings like that, man versus man, woman against woman, all just because that one person wants to get relief for an overwhelmingly compelling biological urge that was primal at the core. Even though she knew she couldn't stay in the bathroom forever, the fact that she was now done and she was making those other women wait was kind of making her satisfied. The longer she stayed in there the longer before any of them could use the bathroom. They made her blink, and now she was going to make them blink.

Jill took her sweet time in the bathroom sitting down on the seat and simply whistling to herself. Finally she heard someone pounding on the bathroom door and shouting for her to open up.

Finally she knew she could wait no longer, so she opened the door and as soon as she did the three women from before practically were knocking each other over to get into the bathroom. Jill could see there was an entire stampede of people going towards the bathroom, so she slowly but surely pushed her way through the crowd and over to her four friends.

"You're just lucky everybody else had to go to the bathroom badly as well," Ashley said. "I think we had better get out of here while we still can."

And with that the five of them slowly and carefully snuck out of the bar, got to the car and got the hell out of there.

5

When Jill finally got home from the bladder buster at the bar she had to admit that she was completely and utterly exhausted. Holding a very full bladder all day really takes a lot of energy out of you, and she knew that her bladder was going to be really sore that night.

Jill's bladder was so sensitive that as soon as she got home she immediately went to the bathroom again. She felt like she didn't get it all out while she was at the bar and she found herself peeing quite intensely considering that she had just gone not that long ago.

Jill decided that she would take a long bath and that she

would really soak, soak her bladder specifically. She rubbed the area of her bladder with soothing bath oils hoping that maybe that would help to take away some of the soreness and irritation in her bladder.

"I don't know how I'm going to deal with this job," Jill said as she sat there soaking and rubbing her bladder with the bath oils. But as Jill continued rubbing her sore bladder with the bath oil she couldn't help but feel a little bit aroused and soon found her fingers going a little bit lower and lower until she found herself masturbating furiously.

When she dried off and looked at herself in the mirror she had to admit that she felt some degree of excitement but a large degree of rage. She hated the fact that as horrible as that experience was it was also extremely arousing, which made it even more embarrassing, and the prospect of going through it again at work tomorrow even more intimidating.

Jill decided that she would go to bed early that night but found herself having to get up to go to the bathroom and then that made her want to masturbate more. She was furious at how arousing the whole situation was. She had to admit that really unfair and brutal situations like that were perhaps the most exciting and arousing sexually, even though she would do virtually anything possible to avoid them in reality.

But as she drifted off to sleep she knew that wouldn't be the case, she knew that tomorrow at work it would be the same exact situation, another day of agonizing bladder pain while all of her friends and coworkers enjoyed the luxury of having a bathroom no more than a few feet away.

"Dammit how could they see that as anything other than extremely unfair?!" Jill shouted and once again she couldn't help but get a little bit of tingling through her body when she thought of just how unfair it was, and how much that was frustrating her. She would have to masturbate again.

That night Jill had a restless sleep. She woke up several times to go to the bathroom with vague memories of dreams where she was looking for a bathroom but not finding one. Those dreams were relatively common for her, but these had an intensity that her dreams normally didn't have. It's like her subconscious was terrified at the prospect of another day without a bathroom, but also excited and titillated by the possibility, not just the possibility, the inevitability. She knew that no matter what she did that tomorrow she would be suffering agonizing bladder pain by the end of the day again, she could pretty much count on it.

After Jill woke up the next morning and took her shower she decided that she would have a really light breakfast and that she would skip the orange juice, since it tended to make her have to go to the bathroom. She wasn't sure what it was about orange juice but it tended to irritate her bladder.

As Jill sat on the toilet a few minutes before her friends arrived she tried to get out every last drop of urine in her body until she was actively pushing it out, causing her to have to do more than pee, but she thought that was for the best anyway, as she wanted to get everything out of her. She knew that it would be the last time she would be going to the bathroom until the end of the day, at which point her bladder would be absolutely screaming for release.

On top of everything else Jill knew that she would probably be in an even worse situation because her bladder was still irritated from the day before, so she would probably end up having to pee more than usual while she was at work, which was exactly what she didn't want.

As her friends pulled up to take her to work she got in the back seat with Patricia and Leah, but it seemed like nobody really wanted to say anything. They all knew what the situation was but it seemed like it was rude of any of them to address the elephant in the room, the fact that they knew that while they were at work they would be able to go to the bathroom whenever they wanted and she would not.

As they got out of the car and went to the office Jill decided she would take one last opportunity to use the bathroom before they drove her over to the warehouse, because even though she used the bathroom right before leaving the house she figured every last little bit counted. Even just another 15 or 20 minutes less off the last time she went to the bathroom would help as the day went on.

Jill looked around at the bathroom in the office and she had to admit it was pretty damn nice. She could see why Ashley was singing the praises of this place. If only she had a bathroom like that in the warehouse. She still couldn't understand how it could be considered a business expense to provide a bathroom, a very necessary room, in the warehouse. Why couldn't they spring for a bathroom for her? They gave this wonderful bathroom to all of her coworkers and she had to basically just sit there in the warehouse not peeing all day. She couldn't help but get another frustration high thinking about it.

Jill slowly came out of the bathroom and walked over to where the rest of her coworkers were. She couldn't help but overhear some of their conversation.

"So that was crazy with Jill the other day wasn't it," Samantha said.

"What do you mean," Leah said, knowing very well what Samantha was referring to.

"She went all day without using the bathroom even once!" Samantha said.

"Big deal we've been doing that every day," Patricia said. "I don't understand why anyone would use a bathroom at work."

Samantha laughed.

"What's so funny?" Patricia asked.

"What, are you serious," Samantha said. "Most people have to go to the bathroom at some point during the day."

"Well I guess we're not most people," Leah said as she nodded at Patricia and smiled. "Some of us prefer to hold it all day rather than use a public restroom."

"Is that why Jill didn't go to the bathroom all day?" Samantha asked as Leah and Patricia burst out laughing. "What's so funny?"

"Trust me if Jill had a bathroom she would have been using it frequently," Patricia said. "Personally I think that the situation is just perfect. We were always telling Jill that she went to the bathroom too much and relied too much on public toilets, and now she has to go all day without one, so I guess it will teach her to just hold it in better."

"For six hours?!" Samantha shouted. "That's pretty brutal."

Patricia shook her head. "No, I think any adult who can't go six hours without using the bathroom should probably go to a urologist or something, because there is clearly something wrong with them. You should be able to hold it for six or eight hours or more. I usually only go once a day and I only go at home, I certainly wouldn't subject my ass to sitting on a public toilet seat that has been sat upon by dozens of women."

"As crazy as it sounds, that sounds almost like some degree of bathroom snobbery or something," Samantha said shaking her head. "I know that I can't go six hours a day without a bathroom, do you think something is wrong with me?"

Patricia shook her head. "I didn't mean it like that; I think it's actually fairly typical."

"What is fairly typical?" Samantha said seemingly confused.

"Most people just go to the bathroom the first second that they feel the slightest urge to go and that's why nobody ever builds up bladder strength. People just don't use their bladder for its intended purpose, holding it in."

Samantha shook her head again. "You don't think it's the least bit unfair that we have access to a bathroom and Jill has to go all day without a bathroom? Clearly she was very uncomfortable yesterday, and I felt like I should say something except, well."

"Except what?" Patricia asked.

Samantha blushed and sort of giggled. "It's nothing, it's just, I know it makes me sound like a bitch and everything, but it was kind of funny, almost entertaining even to see Jill squirming around all day. Just watching how she managed to cope with all of that, well I don't know what it was, but it certainly wasn't boring!"

Leah put her hand on Samantha's shoulder. "You don't need to say anything, we understand, and don't worry there's nothing weird about it."

"There isn't?" Samantha said looking relieved.

Leah shook her head. "No, there's nothing weird about it, you are probably just empathizing with her is all."

"Yeah, I probably just empathize because I have been in that situation before," Samantha said. "I think that every woman has been in a situation where she was unable to go to the bathroom for a while. Like this last office I worked at they were renovating the ladies rooms and we really didn't have any place to go to the bathroom. It was really awful because we would have to wait until our lunch break and then find somewhere in town or somewhere nearby to go to the bathroom. By the time lunch came around I was about as squirmy and uncomfortable as Jill was yesterday. It was a difficult couple of weeks and I have no idea how I got through it, much like I don't know how Jill is getting through this right now, it must be driving her crazy, don't you think?"

Patricia shook her head. "Don't worry about Jill, she'll be fine, I think that she could afford to do some holding. Maybe this will teach her some better self-control and not to go running to the bathroom at the first slight urge. I certainly didn't get a huge bladder overnight; I spent my entire childhood training for it."

"Training for it?" Samantha said shaking her head and smiling and laughing. "You make it sound like you were training for the Olympics or something. Most people when they say they are training they're training for a sport or something."

"The bladder Olympics," Leah said as she and Patricia laughed. "If there were such a thing I can guarantee that Patricia here would definitely be a gold medalist, no weird pun intended there."

"I could totally go national," Patricia said with a laugh. "I guess I just got tired of letting my bladder dictate my life. When I was younger I would have to go to the bathroom and the thought of using some type of public toilet was just disgusting, so over time I trained myself to hold it, and now I can go basically all day without having to use a bathroom anywhere but home."

"Don't you feel like you need to go though?" Samantha said. "I mean I take a couple of drinks and I have to go pretty badly usually."

"You've got to play through the pain," Patricia said. "There is certainly nothing wrong with holding a full bladder for as long as possible."

"Yeah but isn't it kind of dangerous to hold it that much, because maybe you could do damage to your bladder," Samantha said. "You could get a urinary tract infection or you could sprain your bladder or do some type of damage and then end up springing leaks when you are older. I'm just saying that you don't want to abuse your bladder too much."

"Most people don't give their bladder enough of a workout," Patricia said. "Lazy bladders."

"Well you have to do everything in moderation, I mean I hold it all day but I haven't had any bladder problems," Leah said.

Samantha shrugged his shoulders. "I just heard that it's good to let it all come out and let the bladder release when it needs it."

"Where did you hear that?" Patricia said. "It was on the Internet wasn't it? But you know what they say about the Internet, as Abe Lincoln said you can't always trust everything that you read on the Internet."

All of them had a good laugh at that as Jill continued listening secretly.

"Hey Jill are you ready for me to take you down to the warehouse," Kate said as she tapped her on the shoulder.

Jill was startled but she turned around and saw Kate and nodded. "Yeah, I guess I am ready."

Jill didn't say much as Kate drove her over to the warehouse, but when she finally got there and opened up the warehouse to let Jill inside to go to her station, Jill hesitated a moment.

"Is something the matter Jill?" Kate asked.

Jill was normally not one to complain, especially when she was at her second day on a new job like that, which was paying her a lot better than her previous job, but she found it hard to hold it inside, no pun intended.

"Kate," Jill said as Kate started walking away.

"Yes Jill, what is it?" Kate said looking annoyed to be kept waiting.

"I was just wondering if there's any possibility that maybe you will install a bathroom in the warehouse at some point," Jill said as meekly as possible hoping that maybe it would garner her some sympathy.

Kate frowned and shook her head. "I'm sorry Jill but it just wouldn't be practical, we would have to install a plumbing system in the warehouse, and we would have to find some place to put the bathroom when there really isn't any place, and it's just not cost-effective. Besides you signed a contract saying that you accepted the conditions of the warehouse as being less than stellar. It's just not a requirement for us to have a bathroom in the warehouse when it's all out of the way like this. Now I think it's time for you to get to work as I have a lot of stuff to do back at the other office."

The other office, the one with bathroom access whenever you needed it, Jill thought to herself, but she could see that Kate did not seem to be very sympathetic to her condition.

"Kate I just have one more question," Jill said as Kate turned around once again looking annoyed.

"What is it Jill?" Kate said as she folded her arms in a really authoritative and agitated manner.

"I'm just curious but who was in the warehouse before I had the job?"

"Well Jill it was actually a guy named Jack, Jack and Jill it would seem."

"And before that?"

"I don't really remember, I think it was Joe, Bob, just a whole bunch of guys. Why, does it really matter?"

"No, I was just curious; I guess I'll get busy at my job then."

As Kate left Jill finally had confirmation of what she thought, it was, in Kate's own words, "a whole bunch of guys" who were in the warehouse before her, and she had no doubt that that coffee can got lots of good mileage from them.

"No way am I using that," Jill said as she looked at the coffee can sitting in the corner of the room and stuck out her tongue with disgust.

It didn't take Jill long to get to work because as soon as she turned on her monitor she had a whole bunch of inventory to check out for her fellow coworkers. Jill tried to drink as little as possible, despite the fact that it was really hot and stuffy in the warehouse. She figured that the less she drank the less possibility of a bathroom emergency. However as she considered that possibility she also had to admit that the prospect that she was going to see a repeat of yesterday was also a little bit exciting. Her job was a little bit monotonous, and that bathroom emergency she had yesterday did put a little bit of excitement into the day. Of course she didn't really want that to happen again, but her mind kept racing with those thoughts every time she had a spare moment to herself to contemplate things.

Keeping liquids to a minimum seemed to be having the desired effect. Two hours into her job Jill found that she wasn't yet really bursting to go to the bathroom like she often was. However as the day went on she found herself getting thirstier and thirstier and couldn't help but drink some of her water and her juice.

By the time lunch came around, even though she wasn't as desperate as she was yesterday, her bladder was still sore and she still had to go to the bathroom.

Jill quickly ate her lunch, and although she didn't want to drink too much, her lunch made her thirsty, so she couldn't help but drink most of the juice that she had brought. She started to walk around the warehouse looking it over. She had to admit that as much as she didn't want to admit it, Kate did have a point. The warehouse was just a big empty place full of rows and rows of inventory, and they just sort of stuck a desk in there for her. She didn't really see any place where they could install a bathroom.

. In fact the warehouse was almost kind of like an aircraft carrier or a hanger of some kind. The building was mostly made of metal and there wasn't any evidence of a place where they could put in any type of running water. It made Jill a little bit depressed to think that she had this really nice office, or rather her coworkers had a really nice office and bathroom, and she was relegated to working in the warehouse.

She realized that she had agreed to this and the pay was better, but she really would have liked a bathroom. She felt that if she had a time machine and could go back on it she would not have taken the job. She would have preferred to be working in the nice office with all of her friends and coworkers, going to the bathroom whenever she damn well pleased.

At the same time however she felt like she had something to prove to Patricia and Leah. She knew that if she showed signs that she was desperate that she would never hear the end of it. She started to feel even a little bit cocky and arrogant, haughty even. She was determined to prove to them that she could get through the day without letting her bladder rule her life.

Easier said than done.

In spite of the fact that she limited her liquid intake as much as possible, by the fourth hour she was definitely feeling heaviness in her bladder. As she looked at the clock and realized that she still had two hours left she couldn't help but frown.

Once again she couldn't help but notice that Samantha just came back from the bathroom with her face virtually beaming with a big smile and everything. Jill also noticed that she hadn't even been paying attention but that she had already instinctively crossed her legs and was shaking her leg a little bit.

"Hey Jill how are you doing," Samantha said still smiling. Jill almost thought that she was kind of smirking even.

"I'm doing okay," Jill said. "Thanks for asking."

"Jill," Samantha said still with a big smile on her face. "I think I need you to get that water pistol."

"Water pistol?" Jill said.

"You know the one that squirts water," Samantha said as she made sort of hissing noises.

"I'll check," Jill said as she got up and started waddling over to the inventory. Samantha couldn't help but smile as she saw Jill clearly crossing her legs while she was standing there looking through the inventory. In fact it was hard for her not to stare at Jill as she sort of squirmed and crossed and uncrossed her legs without even realizing that she was doing it probably.

Finally Jill came over with the water pistol.

"You got it!" Samantha said with a smile. "Maybe you should squirt it to see if it works."

"You mean take it out of the packaging?" Jill asked seemingly puzzled. "Why would we have to test to see if it's working?"

"Don't you just want to squirt all over the place," Samantha said barely able to suppress laughter.

"Are you joking?" Jill asked.

"Yes," Samantha said as she burst out laughing.

"Ha ha very funny," Jill said shaking her head.

"I'm sorry, I couldn't resist."

"No I get it, it's totally hilarious that I can't use a bathroom."

"Sorry Jill I didn't mean to be mean to you like that, it was just so hard to resist." Samantha continued laughing.

"Anything else," Jill asked, feeling rather annoyed.

"No," Samantha said, shaking her head. "I just can't believe that you are able to put up with this all day honestly. Don't you have to go to the bathroom really bad? I mean look how you are sitting!"

That was when Jill suddenly felt really self-conscious over the fact that it was obvious to Samantha that she had to go to the bathroom. Jill hadn't even noticed how tightly her legs were crossed, and that was when it became even more apparent to her that she had to go to the bathroom and that she really had to go pretty bad.

"I hadn't noticed the way I was sitting," Jill said as she uncrossed her legs and tried to sit more professionally but that just put more pressure on her bladder and caused her to wince a little bit.

"Well it really does suck that you don't have a bathroom all day Jill, I'm sorry for you," Samantha said. Jill could see that she was still trying to suppress smiles.

"If you're sorry how come you're smiling," Jill said now getting rather annoyed. "Do you need anything else?"

Samantha started listing a lot of things for Jill to get from the inventory. They didn't address the fact that she had to go to the bathroom really bad for the rest of the day, but Jill knew that even if Samantha felt bad for her that she seemed to be enjoying every moment of it. Every time Jill got up to get another thing from the warehouse inventory she couldn't help but notice that Samantha was staring at her and smiling.

She felt really awkward when towards the end of the day she could barely sit still, and seeing her coworkers all going to the bathroom whenever they needed it just made it worse. Despite the fact that she had limited her liquid intake by the end of the day she was absolutely ready to explode, just like yesterday, and her aching bladder was still as sore as ever.

"Jill I am going to be a couple of minutes late," Kate said on the video monitor. "I'll come pick you up in a little while, I hope you don't mind a little bit of a wait."

"No, of course not," Jill said as she slumped down in her chair and couldn't help but let out an aggravated groan. She had already been waiting all day and she didn't want to wait a single minute longer.

Finally Kate arrived another 15 or 20 minutes later and brought Jill back over to the other office where her friends were waiting in the parking lot outside the building.

"Hey Jill, how was work," Patricia said hardly able to disguise her pleasure at seeing Jill standing there with her legs crossed.

"Get me home as fast as possible!" Jill shouted.

Henry drove as quickly as possible and although no one was saying anything Jill could see that all of her friends, who were now her coworkers, all seemed like they were a lot more relaxed than she was, and she couldn't help but notice that they all had big smiles on their faces.

This is the second day of the rest of my life, Jill thought to herself, as they finally pulled up in front of her house.

As soon as they pulled up in front of her house Jill ran out of the car without even saying goodbye to her friends, fumbled with her keys for a moment, practically kicked down the door, just narrowly missed tripping on her cat, ran into the bathroom, didn't even take time to close the door, jerked down her skirt, slammed her ass down on the toilet and basically exploded.

Jill let out a loud moan of relief as she sat back on the toilet. At that moment she had such a massive orgasm that she felt like she was about to fall right off the toilet.

Although she hated herself for it, as soon as she was done in the bathroom she went to her room, got undressed, sat down on her bed and masturbated furiously to thoughts of her day at work until she practically passed out.

She knew that she would sleep well that night.

6

Jill never thought that she would get used to this so quickly, which is exactly because she didn't quite get used to it. But when she woke up on the fifth day of work that morning she could already start feeling the soreness in her bladder from the last couple of days.

She knew it wasn't a good sign when she woke up and she

felt soreness in her bladder. She had done some holds before under controlled circumstances, but that was always at home where the bathroom was just a few moments away, and when she wanted to throw in the towel she could. Now that she had no option but to continue holding at work and no possible outlet for relief she wasn't holding out of choice, she was holding out of necessity, and that was really straining her bladder.

In fact she was finding that in the morning she didn't even really want to have breakfast because she knew that having breakfast would just make her thirsty, and that drinking would fill her bladder, and that filling her bladder would make her job more difficult. It really was something of a vicious cycle. She knew she had to stay hydrated but she also wanted to try to minimize the amount of bladder pain she had during work hours. She knew that even if she was really careful by the end of the day regardless she would be pretty much close to exploding.

As Jill went into the bathroom that morning to take a shower she pulled down her pants and looked at her bladder region. Nothing looked out of place and it didn't look like she had swollen it or done any damage. But she could definitely still feel soreness when she touched it, and she also found herself peeing really forcefully when she did go. She didn't pee at work all day but then when she got home she made up for it by peeing more often than usual. She figured if she had to hold it at work she should give her bladder as much of a break as possible when she was at home.

She also couldn't deny however that having a full bladder all day was also making her extremely horny. That was exactly what she didn't really want to have to deal with at work. Aside from the fact that she already had to deal with an aching full bladder, the fact that it also made her hot and bothered and that it also made her coworkers, or at least a couple of them anyway she knew, hot and bothered, made the whole situation even more awkward and tense.

"I never thought I would have a job where I am both in agonizing pain and horny out of my mind at the same time and somehow still have to work under those conditions," Jill said as she peed loudly in the toilet.

When Jill's coworkers came up to pick her up in the carpool

that morning they mostly made small talk in the car. Once again she couldn't help but notice that nobody really wanted to address the elephant in the room. They all knew that when they got to work Jill would be desperate by the end of the day, and that they would be watching her every move like they were a movie crew, but she figured that probably none of them wanted to say it because that would just make things even more awkward between them.

The other thing though that she didn't really like was the fact that it took such a short amount of time for this whole unfair system of bladder brutality to become normalized. On the first day everyone was shocked at the idea that Jill would have to work all day without a bathroom, and even on the second day people seemed to be at least mildly sympathetic, but now that she was approaching the last day of her first full week people had other concerns other than the fact that one of their coworkers was doing their job while also doing the bathroom jitterbug.

At the same time though Jill felt that maybe Patricia and Leah had developed some type of newfound respect for her, as did her other friends and coworkers. They had always teased her about her small bladder and how she wasn't able to hold it, but now she had proved every day that week that if she really was forced to she could hold it all day just like they could, albeit not as easily as they did.

Really the difference between their situations couldn't be starker. While Leah and Patricia were holding it because they enjoyed every last minute of it, and because they didn't want to go to the bathroom at work, they did so mostly comfortably. While they were working throughout the day they showed no actual signs of desperation, even though she knew that they must have had to go to the bathroom just as badly as she did. But they probably didn't feel it as acutely as she did because they were used to holding it, she was not.

Pretty much as soon as they arrived at the office Jill ran immediately for the bathroom. She knew that Patricia and Leah were probably rolling their eyes at her the entire time when she did that, even though she just went to the bathroom before leaving her house. But Jill realized that even one last bathroom break 15 or 20 minutes later still made a difference towards the end of the day. It may not seem significant when you are holding it for six hours but there is still a very noticeable difference between holding it for six hours and then an additional 15 or 20 minutes before that, and she could feel the difference by the end of the day.

As Jill came out of the bathroom she couldn't help but notice all of the coworkers looking up, and a few of them were clearly smiling. Once again she wasn't sure if they were smiling because they enjoyed seeing her suffer or because they genuinely admired how she was grinning and bearing so much excruciating bladder pain throughout the day. Jill didn't want to use the word hero, because it made her sound like an egotistical bitch, but she almost felt like what she was doing at this point was heroic.

Never in a million years would she tell Leah or Patricia that she thought she deserved some type of gold medal simply because she managed to hold it in for a couple of hours. They would simply point out that they have been doing that for basically forever, so if she got a medal for doing it once they should be getting a medal for it every single day.

As Jill waited for Kate to come by to drop her off at the warehouse for the day she even thought that maybe she should have lingered in the bathroom longer, even another five minutes could make a difference by the end of the day, but then she thought she was just being obsessive compulsive, like she was when she was a child and had to repeatedly go to the bathroom several times before leaving a place because she wanted to make sure she got every last drop out. She knew that Patricia and Leah would say that that was the reason why she never developed good bladder control in the first place, so she didn't like to bring up that detail from her past.

But while she was waiting for Kate she sometimes tried to listen in on conversations between her coworkers to see if they were talking about her situation, and it made her feel somewhat narcissistic to think that her bladder was so interesting that it would be the talk of the town, but she figured if she wasn't there maybe in hushes and whispers her coworkers would express some type of secret sympathy for her, or consequently a secret sadism. For some reason the later sounded like it would be more exciting to her.

Although she didn't expect that she would hear anything again like she did the other day, she was genuinely surprised and delighted to see that people were actually talking about her, not knowing that she was on the other side of the wall listening in on their conversations like some type of spy or secret agent.

"So are we just like going to pretend that this is normal," Samantha said.

"Pretend that what is normal?" Leah asked.

"I mean the whole Jill situation," Samantha said. "Certainly I'm not the only one who thinks it a bit strange that we are just talking to her throughout the workday and having her go get stuff for us and watching her as she crosses her legs and give us that look of absolute agony every time she has to get up. Is it just me or does something seem not quite so right about that?"

"I've already accepted it as normal," Christina said as she came over.

"That's good, that's what we should all do," Patricia said. "I can say that there is absolutely nothing abnormal about not going to the bathroom all day."

"But did you see her; she's clearly going out of her mind by the end of the day!" Samantha said. "I feel like maybe we should say something or do something."

"Well if Jill's not going to say anything then I don't think that we should," Christina said. "We just have to assume that she is fine with the situation."

"Is she though?" Samantha asked. "Generally when someone is walking around on tip toes and stopping every few minutes to cross their legs and grab themselves they aren't exactly comfortable. I don't know if I could ever possibly work under the conditions that Jill works under."

Patricia shook her head. "Don't worry about Jill, she's a trooper. Like I said I think that this is a good thing for her, she is finally learning to let her bladder do its natural job and hold it during the day. I have been doing this for years and I don't see anything wrong with it."

"Yeah but you don't want to become incontinent or something when you are older do you?" Samantha said. "I know that sometimes people who hold it excessively can do damage to their bladder over the long term. Just going one day without a bathroom break isn't going to kill a person, but over a long stretch of time you are stretching out the bladder in an unhealthy way. You could get urinary tract infections, you could pull a muscle in your bladder, or like I said when you get older maybe you won't be able to hold it as well. Sure you can hold it really great now, but over time you might be weakening the bladder rather than strengthening it. It just doesn't seem like it's really good for your health."

"Nonsense," Patricia said. "I have been holding it for years and I have not noticed any ill effects. The only effect that I have noticed is that I can get through the day without having to worry about running to the nearest bathroom every five minutes, and I think that that's something everyone should aspire to. If you gradually start holding it more and more, well then eventually your capacity will increase, and I have no doubt that that's what's going to happen to Jill."

"I don't know if it's so gradual though," Samantha said. "Suddenly she is now in a situation where she has no bathroom all day, was that normal for her before?"

Henry and Ashley came by and they started laughing along with Leah and Patricia as they all simultaneously said no before laughing again.

"This seems like you're being kind of cruel to your friend," Samantha said. "I mean I teased her a little bit and everything, I'm only human, but it seems like this could have some type of really long-term negative effect, I mean both physically and psychologically."

Patricia said. "Like I said, a little pee holding never seriously hurt anyone, so I'm not worried."

Patricia patted Leah on the shoulder as Leah sort of nodded and half smiled, but she had to admit to herself there was something about Samantha's words that was starting to ring true to her. She had always held it all day long but sometimes by the end of the day she also had to go quite badly. Maybe she didn't have to go as badly and desperately as Jill did, but she did in the back of her mind occasionally wonder if she was doing damage to her health in the long term, and thought that maybe she should sometimes cool it and give her bladder a rest.

"Hey Jill are you ready to go to the warehouse now," Kate said as she came up behind Jill and startled her while she was eavesdropping on her friends.

Jill nodded, and as Kate led her away from her coworkers she couldn't help but notice that they were looking at her. Did they know that she had been eavesdropping; now she was going to feel even more awkward about that. She felt like she was privy to a conversation about herself that perhaps she shouldn't have overheard.

Once Jill got to the warehouse the day pretty much fell into its normal routine. Jill tried to limit her liquid intake so that her bladder wouldn't be in agony the entire day, but she knew that by the last two hours of the day she would be feeling awfully uncomfortable, no matter what the case may be.

She was starting to get used to her job, even if she still felt it was extremely unfair. Every time one of her coworkers got up to go to the bathroom she had to admit that she kind of wanted to slap them. It was almost like a slap to her bladder every time one of her coworkers used the bathroom, especially when they were on videoconference together. She thought that they could at least be polite enough not to rub it in her face that they had bathroom access when she didn't.

But Jill was not the confrontational type. Even though she knew that her coworkers were probably noticing her state of despair, she also felt that aside from her friends that most of them had probably already considered it normal. It really is kind of crazy when she thought about it, just the type of things that we normalize. She thought that this insanity was mostly in politics and religion, but even in the simpler situation of office politics people also tended to normalize things that they should not.

Certainly Jill thought that her coworkers should be more concerned over the fact that she didn't have a bathroom, and she was glad that she overheard that at least some of them were talking about it. So even if it was already normalized that this was just the way things were, at least some other people in the office realized that something was simply not right about the situation.

At the same time however she realized that nobody was speaking up or doing anything about it, and whenever she brought up the topic of the bathroom to Kate it would always be dismissed. She figured that she signed her contract and it was pretty much the same as selling her soul to the bladder devil. Maybe she would find some solution around that someday, but for now she would just have to grin and bear it and do her job the best she could.

By the fourth hour, as usual, her bladder was feeling incredibly full. She wasn't to the point where she was in agony or pain or anything, but it was definitely to the point where she couldn't sit comfortably and ignore it. She was already sitting with her legs crossed, and she knew that she had at least two hours left before the day was over, and those were always the hardest two hours of the day.

Jill very slowly and carefully sipped one of her drinks, but once again she didn't want to drink too much, only enough that she wouldn't get dehydrated or anything like that in the warm and stuffy environment of the warehouse. She started to wonder herself if this was worth the slight increase in pay. Once again she wished that she had a time machine and could go back and change things so that she would be in the nice office right now, and maybe one of her friends would be suffering in the warehouse instead, which she had to admit was a nice thought. That made her feel kind of evil, but she knew that if Leah or Patricia had been in the warehouse they wouldn't even have minded it.

That was one of the other things that really got to her. Firstly there was the fact that she needed a bathroom and didn't have it, but then there was the double whammy of the fact that her friends had access to a bathroom, and at least two of them never even needed it. They could easily have gone through the bladder busting job of working in the warehouse without even breaking a sweat or shrugging a shoulder or batting an eyelash at the idea of it, and yet they were the ones who had the bathroom access and she did not. She was the one who needed it and didn't have it, and her friends who didn't need it but had access to it. She always said that it's always better to have something and not need it than need something and not have it, and right now she definitely needed a bathroom and her friends did not, and yet they were the ones who had it.

Today Jill was mostly conferencing with Leah towards the end of the day. The one good thing about talking to her as opposed to her other friends and coworkers is that with her and Patricia at least that she knew there was no possibility, hardly an ice cube's chance in hell, that they would ever get up to go to the bathroom and relieve themselves while videoconferencing with Jill. That was an added torture that she did not need.

At the 4 1/2 hour mark Jill realized that she still had a full 90 minutes to go, and already she was squirming in her seat. She felt that with each day that she was holding it that her bladder got antsy sooner and sooner, but the day didn't get any shorter as a result of that.

But that was the moment when something happened that Jill never thought that she would see happening, the very thing that was the last thing in the world that she wanted to see.

"Jill do you think you can excuse me for a moment," Leah said.

"Where are you going?" Jill asked.

"I'll be back in a moment, don't worry, I'll be quick about it," Leah said as she got up and left the video call.

"Where on earth is she going?" Jill said shaking her head. Jill watched Leah on the video monitor and that was when Leah walked over to the office bathroom, opened the door and walked inside.

"Where did Leah go?" Patricia said on the video monitor.

"I think she went to the bathroom," Jill found herself saying, barely able to form the words.

"Very funny, now where did she go really," Patricia said.

"She went to the bathroom," Samantha said. "Maybe my talk earlier had gotten to her."

Patricia shook her head. "Why on earth would Leah go to the bathroom when she is going to be home in another two hours anyway?"

"Everybody has a bathroom emergency sometimes," Samantha said shrugging her shoulders. "In fact I hope she is quick because as soon as she gets back I think that I'm going to need to go."

"What the hell, are you all having a pee party in there or something?" Jill said as she shook her leg in agitation.

"When you gotta go you gotta go," Samantha said as she looked at Jill. "Well I mean if the bathroom is there and everything."

"Samantha," Jill said forcing a smile.

"Yes Jill," Samantha said as she smiled back.

"Please shut up!" Jill shouted as she pressed her heel down on the top of her other foot.

"Okay," Samantha said as she saw Leah coming back. "Well off I go!"

Jill made sort of a low growling noise, practically grinding her teeth together, as she saw Samantha waddle off leisurely towards the bathroom just a few feet away.

"Okay I'm back," Leah said as she sat back down smiling.

"What the hell was that?" Jill asked.

"What are you talking about?"

"You know exactly what the hell I am talking about, where you went."

"So I went to the bathroom, do have a problem with that?"

"Really, you're actually asking me that right now," Jill said her legs tightly crossed and her one leg shaking 100 miles a second as Jill gripped the edge of her seat like she was in pain.

Leah shook her head and shrugged her shoulders. "Hey Jill it's a free country, if I have to go to the bathroom am allowed to go to the bathroom."

"Well I'm not allowed to go to the bathroom!" Jill said practically whimpering.

Once again Leah shrugged her shoulders and shook her head. "Well hey Jill we all have our own problems I suppose. If you didn't want to work without a bathroom you shouldn't have signed up for the warehouse job, so I guess you'll just have to learn to live with your decision."

"But you never go to the bathroom," Jill said shaking her head in astonishment.

"Well hey today I did, and I feel a lot better for it," Leah said with something of a smug smile as she crossed her arms over her chest.

"What the hell is going on here?" Jill asked shaking her head. "Have I entered bizarro world or something? Are you going to make this a habit or something?"

"Jill I just used the bathroom, stop freaking out about it," Leah said but Jill could tell from the look on Patricia's face that she thought something was wrong as well.

"I mean are you okay and everything?" Jill asked.

Leah laughed. "Jill just because I went to the bathroom doesn't mean that there is something wrong with me, people go to the bathroom you know."

"Yeah but not you, you never go to the bathroom at work!"

Leah once again shrugged her shoulders. "Well hey today I did, and you know what, it felt pretty damn good. But now if we could get back to the matter at hand I need you to check the inventory for a couple of things."

Jill felt kind of infuriated for a moment that Leah had just shot down their conversation like that. She was even more infuriated by the fact that Leah was giving her orders from the standpoint of a person with an empty bladder.

For the rest of the day Jill didn't say anything and neither did any of her other coworkers, but she could feel the tension in the air. She couldn't help but think that Leah was being a little bit more bossy and smirking a lot during the day. Jill felt like she almost went to the bathroom just to spite her or something. She knew she was probably being paranoid and that she shouldn't be mad over her friend performing a natural biological function like that, but she couldn't deny that she was really annoyed by it.

By the end of the day, as always, Jill felt that her bladder was about ready to explode.

"Jill I just need you to check one more thing, do you think you can do that," Leah said.

"But the day is over," Jill said as she sat there shaking in her seat tapping her legs rapidly.

"I wasn't asking," Leah said as she shook her head and frowned.

Jill almost felt like muttering a curse word under her breath but she did as Leah asked as she waddled over to the inventory, stopping every few moments to pause and cross her legs.

"Hurry up Jill," Leah said. "It's already after hours."

"Just a second," Jill said as she got the inventory, which seemed to satisfy Leah.

"Thanks Jill, I will see you in a couple of minutes," Leah said as the videoconference ended and Jill sat down at her desk waiting for Kate to arrive.

Once again Kate took her sweet ass time coming to get Jill, and by the time she had arrived back where her friends were waiting for her she was walking very slowly like she was carrying something between her legs, like she just dropped the load in her pants or something, which she felt she might do if she didn't get home quickly, a very wet load.

She sat down in the back of the car with Leah but neither of them said anything about the events of the day, and in fact everybody was really quiet.

"Henry do you think you could stop at the store a minute, I just need to run in and get something," Leah said.

"I think maybe we should just get home pretty quickly," Jill said now holding herself and shifting in place like crazy.

"Don't be rude Jill, she just needs a minute," Henry said, taking Leah's side and infuriating Jill further.

Leah smiled, once again looking somewhat smug, got out of the car and went into the smoke shop. The rest of them waited in the car but when 10 minutes went by Jill was really starting to get angry.

"She said she was only going to be a minute, we've been waiting 10 minutes!" Jill shouted. Jill was tempted to run out and go into the store and say something and see what was taking her so long, but she also didn't think she could stand up and didn't want to risk a confrontation with her bladder in such an advanced state of fullness.

"Sorry I took so long, there was a line," Leah said as she sat down smiling.

"Well hey, no rush," Ashley said as Jill bit down hard on her lip. At that moment she wanted to scream, she wanted to yell at her friend and let out all of the pent up emotions, but she controlled herself, because there was something else that was really pent up that she wanted to release first and that was a much more urgent need.

Without even saying a word to her friends Jill jumped out of the car, ran towards her front door, practically collided with the door and bumped her head because she was in such a rush, pushed the door open, once again barely missed tripping over the cat, jerked down her skirt and panties, sat her ass on the toilet and screamed at the top of her lungs. "Leah!"

Thank God it's Friday and my bladder finally gets its weekend rest, were Jill's last thoughts before she wiped herself, walked into her bedroom and collapsed onto her bed and fell swiftly asleep.

7

Jill had to admit that she really needed that weekend pretty badly. It was a really exhausting first week at work, not so much for her, but more so for her bladder. She couldn't remember the last time she had had to hold it so much so frequently so many days in a row, and now it was really starting to take a strain on her.

"But this weekend I am giving my bladder the vacation and the rest that it so desperately needs," Jill said as she sat on the toilet and peed very loudly. She couldn't help but notice that she was peeing more forcefully and aggressively when she did go to the bathroom, and when she wasn't at work she found herself going to the bathroom a lot more than usual. She had done some holds for recreational purposes before and sometimes ended up having to pee more after that, but she felt that all of this continuous holding so many days in a row was really starting to take its toll on her bladder, and she was worrying that it was perhaps weakening her bladder over time.

As Jill soaked in the bathtub she started wondering to herself if maybe it wasn't the best idea to take this job in the first place. Of course when she took the job she had no idea that it didn't have bathroom access, because she figured it was pretty much a given that anyplace would have bathroom access for any employee anywhere they went. She was slowly starting to learn that it was not necessarily true; it was not necessarily true at all.

She also couldn't help but continue thinking about Leah and how she had suddenly started going to the bathroom. Jill had never seen Leah go to the bathroom at work or away from home before if she could really help it short of an emergency, but if she started going to the bathroom how did she know Patricia wouldn't be next?

"Actually that's probably not likely," she said with a laugh as she shook her head. Patricia was extremely militant about the idea of not using a bathroom anywhere but home or going more than once a day. Although there were some exceptions it was pretty much a religious observance to not use the bathroom more than once a day. Jill had no idea how she did it, but the best she could figure is that Patricia was secretly some type of superpowered android from the future, or maybe some type of alien who had come to earth and doesn't need to urinate the same way human beings did.

But she did keep going back to Leah. There was something really cocky and arrogant about the fact that she decided to suddenly start using the bathroom, and just at a time when she knew that Jill was deprived of the bathroom. Sure she knew that that annoyed Jill but the fact that she actually did that it at work really shocked her. She never thought that Leah would actually use a public restroom at work, and was starting to wonder if she was doing that simply to torture her.

As Jill got out of the bathtub and dried off she couldn't get that thought out of her head that Leah was in some way messing with her. The question would be whether she would do it again when she returned to work on Monday, and whether she would broach the topic, and if so, how?

Once Jill got out of the bathtub she started googling the effects of holding your bladder to excess. She came across that story of that woman who held her pee too long and her bladder exploded because she wanted to win a Nintendo Wii. Then she came across an article about another woman who didn't pee for a long time and her bladder became swollen and she had to go to the hospital.

"Okay Jill now you are just getting paranoid," she said to herself as she decided it was best to get off the Internet. Sometimes on the weekend she would like to play holding games with her friends but after everything that she had been through this week her bladder desperately needed that rest, and she was going to be sure that it gets it.

Jill we are going to the bar for drinks, want to come? a text message that she got from her friends read. She simply texted back that she wasn't really feeling up for drinking this weekend, and that she thought she would just take it easy. She had no doubt they were probably thinking the same way that she was, that her bladder needed a rest. She figured without even saying that they would know what she meant by that and that no one needed to address that needless elephant in the room.

The rest of the weekend went by uneventfully and Jill was happy to say that she felt that her bladder had recovered to some degree. Sure it was still hurting her a lot, and sure she was still going to the bathroom more than she used to go to the bathroom, but at least after a couple of days without holding it so severely she was starting to feel better and back to normal. But she was wondering what would happen when she returned to work on Monday? She could only assume it would be back to the same old shit, or rather the same old piss, or rather the same old not pissing, and she would be in a world of bladder pain once again. She didn't know if she could actually sustain it over such a long stretch of time but she didn't want to give up her new job or look weak in front of her friends.

She decided that she would just continue grinning and bearing it and hoping for the best. Maybe if she was a diligent worker and didn't complain about it Kate would reward her by deciding to install a bathroom after all.

Jill shook her head. "Yeah right, what universe are you living in? They don't reward you for doing your job by putting in a bathroom in the warehouse." Jill resigned herself to the fact that for the near future at least this was going to be her fate, and that she would just have to find some way to deal with it.

That Monday her friends picked her up for work like usual and they didn't say anything about what had happened on Friday. No one was addressing the elephant in the room, but Jill had to admit that she was feeling kind of snarky as she sat down next to Leah in the car that day.

"So did that lotto ticket win you anything good?" Jill asked.

"What was that?" Leah asked.

"Remember on Friday you stopped at the smoke shop and were 10 minutes buying that lottery ticket, was it really worth it?"

"What, are you asking did I win the lottery over the weekend?" Leah asked as she pointed to herself. "You mean the $150 million jackpot?"

"Yeah that would be the one, you stood in line for a good 10 minutes to get that lottery ticket, so I was figuring that if you didn't win you must be pretty disappointed."

"Well Jill I'm going to work at a blue-collar office job, so what do you think?"

"Hey it's such a great job I figured that maybe you would keep the job even if you did win $150 million, I mean the bathrooms at the office are so great what millionaire could turn those down?"

"Are you still mad because I went to the bathroom?"

"No I'm mad because I didn't get to go to the bathroom."

"I think it would be easier if none of us had to go to the bathroom more than once a day," Patricia said.

"Well we don't all have mutant superhuman powers like you do," Jill said as she shook her head. "I just wonder what's going to be in store at us for work this week."

"Same shit different day," everybody said breaking the tension in the room. Jill couldn't help but think to herself that it wasn't the same shit, or rather the same piss. They were all going to have access to a bathroom while she would not. For them it wasn't any type of major adjustment, but for her working without a bathroom was a huge adjustment to her normal routine of frequent urination as soon as she needed it.

Not much more was said on the car ride over there but they soon arrived at the office and Jill couldn't help but notice that several people in the office looked at her, and some of them seemed to be smiling. She once again thought that maybe there was this global office wide conspiracy where everybody was secretly smirking to themselves over the fact that they had bathroom access when she did not.

That's it, Jill thought to herself, they are all so smug and complacent because they know that they are the ones who have the bathrooms and that she is the one who is being denied it. In fact it probably made them feel elevated and more powerful, the fact that they had Jill as their little errand girl going around and checking the inventory while trying to balance all of the growing pressure in her bladder all day long.

No, now you're just getting incredibly paranoid and bizarre, Jill told herself as she shook her head as Kate arrived to take her to the warehouse where she would be spending the rest of the day, the rest of the day with a growing sensation in her bladder and no bathroom with which to relieve it.

Soon Jill got to work on her daily routine of checking the inventory as all of her friends asked her what was up in the inventory. It was kind of boring and routine, but at least the routine of it helped her to keep attention away from the fact that her bladder was growing larger by the moment. Even by limiting her liquids and trying to focus on other things, by the halfway point of the day Jill couldn't deny the fact that she really would have liked to use a bathroom. In fact she found herself fantasizing about toilets, not even necessarily using toilets, but just the look and feel of various toilets and how nice it felt to park one's tushie on the just right toilet seat.

As the day wore on she sort of started thinking of all the toilets that she had sat upon in her life, some had really soft seats and others really had hard ones. She always liked the soft seat toilets even though they got destroyed more easily from frequent use. Most public ones, well basically all public ones, were the hard variety, but even that would be a nice feeling on her ass right now if only she could just release her urine into the toilet.

It was after lunch, just when the pressure in Jill's bladder was always starting to get really noticeable, that the day took a strange turn that she had not expected, even at a job as strange as this one had been for her so far.

"Jill do we have a black lace bikini," Kim said on the video monitor.

"Sure we do, I'm pretty sure I saw that in the inventory before, let me go check," Jill said as she hobbled over to the inventory area and found the black lace bikini. She had to admit that it looked really attractive but she could never picture herself wearing one of those in a million years, which is why what would happen when she came back was even more surprising. "Okay I've got the black lace bikini," Jill said as she put it down and then held it up on the video.

Kim smiled. "Do you think you could hold it up in front of you?"

"Okay," Jill said. "Is this good?" Jill stood there holding up the bikini up against her body and smiling as Kim smiled back.

"Actually Jill I got kind of a weird request and you can ask Kate about it, because I am totally not lying and this is true, but do you think you could put it on?"

"But what do you mean put it on?" Jill said as she held up the bikini and looked at it more closely.

"What do you mean what do I mean by that, I mean put on the bikini," Kim said.

"Guys seriously, is this some type of a joke?" Jill said as she looked around. "Are you all going to pop out and yell surprise or something?"

Kate suddenly came on the monitor. "Jill how would you like to make a little bit of extra money as a bonus on top of what you are already making for agreeing to work in the warehouse?"

"You mean work in the warehouse that has no bathroom," Jill couldn't help but once again remind Kate of the fact that she didn't have a bathroom.

"Yes Jill, that," Kate said. "Well we have some requests for this bikini but a lot of people are saying that they would like to see what somebody looks like wearing the bikini, and since you are right there in the warehouse we are wondering if maybe you could model it for us."

"You want me to model a bikini, on video, in front of people?" Jill said and she knew that she was probably blushing by that point already.

"Is something the matter Jill?" Kate asked and she could see all of her friends smiling.

"Well I'm a little bit self-conscious, I don't even really like wearing a one piece as that makes me feel kind of awkward," Jill said as she remembered back to that time when the beach when she was going to the bathroom and she had to get completely naked to slip into her one-piece bathing suit, then her cousin decided to play a mean prank on her and run off with her bathing suit, leaving her stranded naked in the stall. Luckily she was able to get it back before anybody saw her, but it was still extremely embarrassing. Her friends always thought that story was extremely funny, especially her British friend she talked to online named Emma who liked the story because like Jill she was very shy and could relate.

"You have nothing to be self-conscious about Jill," Kim said. "I bet you look really awesome. You have a rocking body and you probably look great in that swimsuit, and I think that we all want to see that, as well as all of our viewers at home."

"How many viewers?" Jill asked as her nervousness grew by the moment.

"Probably only a couple of hundred, but it's going to be a live feed to the Internet so the more people who share you the more product that we will sell," Kate said. "And since you are going to model the bikini for us we will give you a percentage of all the sales that we make. What do you say Jill, would you be willing to give it a try? I think a lot of people would be disappointed if you don't want to model the bikini."

Jill was now feeling a lot of peer pressure to go through with it, but as she looked at the bikini she couldn't help but think how skimpy it was compared to what she normally wore. It wasn't quite a thong but at the same time picturing herself wearing nothing but that felt almost like being practically naked.

"But where would I even get changed?" Jill asked. "This warehouse doesn't exactly have that much privacy, or a bathroom, in case I haven't mentioned that before."

"Oh you mentioned that plenty of times Jill, you certainly won't let me forget about it," Kate said. "But you can go get changed behind some of the stacks of inventory. Don't worry nobody will see you as the warehouse is all but abandoned."

"Okay just give me a minute," Jill said as she took the bikini and ran behind a couple of boxes that she felt gave her sufficient privacy. She had to admit that something about this felt really naughty, almost wrong in some way. She could feel her heart racing as she looked at the skimpy little bikini that she was holding in her hands. She had never worn anything like it before, but she didn't really want to let her friends and coworkers down, and the prospect of a bonus that she felt she desperately needed was not something she could pass up.

"The things I do for this job and for money in general," Jill said as she shook her head as she thought of the degrading and objectifying nature of the capitalist system. She was beginning to feel like something of a prostitute, not just because she was putting on a skin show for a bunch of strangers in order to sell skimpy swimwear, but also because she never figured that she would do something like this for money, but here she was, kowtowing to the capitalist system that enslaved everybody.

"But on the good note I could probably afford that new DVD player I have had my eyes on if I get a bonus," Jill said as she slowly slipped out of her clothing. As she stood there buck naked she could feel the goosebumps forming all over her skin and all of her hair standing up on edge. There was something incredibly taboo about the fact that she was now at work and she was standing naked with nothing shielding her from her friends and a video audience, other than a couple of boxes anyway. It was frightening, but in an exciting way, whatever it was it was really getting her adrenaline flowing.

Jill couldn't help but put her hands on her hips and start making a bunch of poses, not that she had a mirror that she could see herself in. But she was actually starting to feel more confident as she sort of danced around naked behind the boxes. But she figured that her friends were probably waiting for her, so she began to go slip into the bikini. When she was finally dressed in the bikini she had to admit she didn't really feel like she was that much more dressed than she was a moment ago, she still felt extremely close to being fully naked in the bikini.

"Don't worry, you look great, either with or without the bikini, even more so without," a man said that she suddenly noticed was standing there.

Jill screamed. "Who are you?!"

"I'm Smithy the janitor, pleased to meet you," he said as he extended his hand as Jill shook it. She couldn't help but notice that he had a huge smile on his face.

"But how long were you standing there?"

"Long enough that you made this the happiest birthday of my life."

Jill screamed once again and almost wanted to slap him, even though she knew it wasn't his fault that he caught her in a state of undress. She had to admit that now her heart was actually racing and there was something exciting and ultimately titillating about it, even though she was completely mortified and humiliated that this creepy old janitor had seen her getting changed into a bikini.

"Okay it's not my birthday, my birthday is in December, but what I just saw will last me a lifetime."

"Get that image out of your head right now!"

Smithy shook his head. "Once you've seen it you can't unsee it, so I will thank you ma'am and I wish you a good day. Now if you'll excuse me I have to go look for that coffee can because I really need to pee!"

The fact that the janitor saw her naked and now was going to get to go to the bathroom was a double whammy that was infuriating Jill, but she knew that if she didn't get back soon her friends would start to wonder where the hell she had gone, and she didn't feel quite like explaining the entire situation to them. In fact she felt like this was something that she most likely would take to her grave.

As she walked over in the bikini she couldn't help but feel again self-conscious as she heard all of her coworkers and friends whistling and hollering at her. She instinctively wanted to cover herself up but she felt that she should be professional and stick to the task at hand.

"Okay I put on the bikini, although I have to admit that I feel a bit drafty in this warehouse now that I think of it, when I usually feel stuffy and warm," Jill said.

"We want you to stand in front of the chair and model the bikini," Kate said. "Strike a few poses, work that body!"

"I'm afraid that I don't know much about modeling swimwear," Jill said. Jill never thought that when she took this job that it would eventually come down to this. Within just one week of working at a swimwear company, in the inventory warehouse no less, she had now been reduced to modeling a bikini for a live web show in order to get people to buy the product. And to think she thought she'd be working in the relative privacy of an office, an office with bathrooms she might add.

As Jill stood there modeling the bikini that was when she suddenly noticed another problem. She couldn't help but feel that as she was standing around and modeling the bikini that the pressure in her bladder was growing more intense. She wasn't used to so much physical motion when her bladder was full, and she was beginning to feel it harder to hold it with every passing moment.

She really started to feel self-conscious when she couldn't deny that she had her legs crossed in a way that she thought made the bathing suit look like it fit better, but really because she was just trying to take the pressure off of her bladder. After another half hour she was pretty much crossing and uncrossing her legs and bending at the knees.

"You are doing great Jill, we are getting a lot likes and shares of this video," Kim said as she could see all of her coworkers were smiling. "I think that they're really enjoying the little dance that you are doing up there."

"What are you talking about, a little dance?" Jill said and that was when she noticed for the first time that she was indeed doing the pee dance. Now she was truly mortified, she couldn't believe that she was up there, and in something as skimpy as that bikini, and doing a pee dance in front of an audience at home. She wanted to stop herself but at the same time she had to go to the bathroom so bad that she could barely stand still.

"This is great, we are selling more of these bikinis than we ever have before," Kate said. "Whatever you are doing up there Jill it's definitely working, keep it up!"

Jill wanted to shout out that what she was doing was trying not to pee herself on video, but she wasn't about to admit that to the world. So she just struggled and continued holding it in and very subtly dancing around, acting like she was simply trying to model the bikini, but realizing that she was being really strategic and trying to keep herself from soaking that bikini, and she didn't mean with water!

"You know right now I feel extremely awkward being the only guy in the office," Henry whispered to Leah in the office. "I think I might have to excuse myself before I have a really embarrassing social situation right now, one that could prove even more embarrassing than the one Jill is finding herself in.

Henry ran into the office restroom, and he knew that it was inappropriate to do at work, but he couldn't help but masturbate just to get it out of his system, as if he didn't he knew that he was going to be having a massive boner, and he didn't want all of the woman at the office to see that. Even before the #MeToo era he knew that that wouldn't fly at work, and for good reason.

Jill was understandably annoyed when she saw Henry come back from the bathroom with a big smile on his face. She thought that it was just because he used the bathroom but she wouldn't realize until later that it was probably more the show that she was putting on for him and all of her other coworkers. She also noticed that her female coworkers seemed to be equally enticed, which made her feel a little bit more self-conscious, but at the same time a little bit flattered and turned on. She liked the idea of thinking that her coworkers might be totally lezing out on her.

But finally the day was almost over and Jill could stop modeling the bikini, and it was just in time too, because she felt like she couldn't put on the show much longer and was worried that she would end up wetting herself, and she didn't want that, even if bikinis were meant to get wet.

"Okay Jill you did well today and you definitely earned that bonus by shaking your moneymaker," Kate said, and as Jill saw her image on the screen he she couldn't help but see Kate seemed to be smirking, as though she really enjoyed putting her through all of that. "But whatever dance you were doing up there it seemed to be really popular with our viewers, as I think that you're going to go viral."

"That's great," Jill said trying to be as sincere as possible but secretly mortified at the idea that there was video of her pee dancing in a bikini out there on the Internet, and a lot of people were probably jerking off to it at that moment. But in some ways maybe she should be flattered, even though she knew it was probably mostly lonely guys, and not a bunch of hot lesbian women who wanted to date her.

"Okay Jill, I guess you can get changed and we will call it a day," Kate said as Jill ran over to behind the boxes where she was really eager to get dressed back in her clothing once again.

For a moment as she was getting undressed she kind of worried that she would end up wetting the bikini. She had to admit that she had peed in her bathing suit before but not when it was dry like that, and this was company property, although she doubted they would sell that particular piece specifically now that she had worn it all day.

As Jill stood there once again dressed she smiled and that was when she noticed Smithy the janitor standing there smiling again.

"How long have you been standing there?" Jill said as she put her hands on her hips and looked at him angrily.

"Enough that you have made this a very happy birthday, as well as a very Merry Christmas, and I say that as someone who's Jewish!"

"Happy Hanukkah then!" Jill shouted as she glared angrily at him as he slinked away awkwardly, as he knew he was guilty.

"My birthday's on Christmas!" he shouted as though that somehow justified it all.

On the drive back to the office Kate repeatedly congratulated Jill on what a good job she had done and told her she could expect a really nice bonus to her check that week, which was something that she looked forward to.

On the car ride home her friends didn't say anything other than making a couple of jokes about Jill doing the dance that dare not speak its name. All of her friends knew what was happening and that made her even more embarrassed by the whole affair.

"But let's just say I did more than pee in the bathroom,"

Henry said as everybody made ewwing noises and laughed.

Jill had to admit that as embarrassing as the whole situation was that she felt exhilarated, mortified and validated at the same time, but as she reached her front door she had to admit that the only thing she felt was that she needed to pee and she needed to pee right then and right there!

As Jill sat on the toilet peeing she couldn't help but think that at least if she had wet herself in that black bikini it probably wouldn't have showed it, and considering how close she came to that, for that she was very thankful. She knew that she would sleep well that night.

8

Jill had to admit to herself that she was pretty much hot and bothered all night long after what had happened at work that day. Something about dancing around desperate to pee trying not to piss herself while in that really lacey skimpy bikini got her really excited. Also the fact that she got caught in a state of undress was also a bit of excitement for her; even though the person who caught her undressed wasn't exactly the person she was hoping to see her like that.

It didn't matter though, because she was feeling absolutely energized by the entire affair. She had never even so much as worn something other than a one piece bathing suit in her entire life, and even then she was usually shy about that, since they were still form fitting. That was the first time she had worn any type of bathing suit in at least several years and it was a very revealing one at that.

Later that night Jill was in her bedroom and she looked at the thing that she had purchased after her friends dropped her off after work; it was her own very skimpy little black bikini. She couldn't picture herself ever wearing that in public again, although in a way she had already worn it in public to a live Internet audience.

"Hey Jill guess who has gone viral," Leah said as she sent her a link on video chat later that night. As Jill watched the video of herself dancing around desperate to pee she couldn't help but once again feel extremely self-conscious. It wasn't just a few people who had seen that, the video had thousands of views on its own, and it had only been one day! Now there was a video circulating of her on the Internet of perhaps one of the most embarrassing situations of her life and she couldn't help but get excited by that.

"Do you think it's really obvious what I am doing?" Jill said.

"You mean the fact that you were dancing around like you are about to piss yourself and rubbing your barely uncovered flesh together like you were trying to start a fire," Leah said as she laughed.

"Maybe only fetishists noticed!"

"Jill, I think you are underestimating people's grasp of the obvious. You don't have to have a fetish for pee desperation to realize that you were doing the bathroom dance like crazy, and you were doing it in a very skimpy outfit that left very little to the imagination. Hell Henry wasn't even able to stay in the room with all of those women because you were getting him so hot and bothered."

"Oh my God, this is so embarrassing," Jill said as she shook her head and placed her palms on her face.

"I don't know, you seem like you are kind of enjoying it. I know that it's extremely embarrassing for you but I also know that embarrassing situations are kind of titillating in their own way. You shared a moment of intimacy with thousands of people over the Internet, hell maybe next you will end up becoming one of those WebCam girls who strips naked on video for people who pay you money for it."

"Hey all I did was model a bikini while I had to pee a little bit, I wasn't exactly running around on a catwalk with tassels twirling on my bare tits!"

"Modeling a bikini while you are absolutely bursting out of your mind and being very very obvious about it." Leah made some tsk tsk tsk motions with her mouth. "It was very unladylike of you Jill."

"Well forgive me if I was suddenly pressured into an awkward situation where I had to pose in a very skimpy bikini and just happened to have to go to the bathroom really bad and tried with all of my force of will to not soak that bikini. This has to be by far the most awkward and embarrassing situation of my life."

"And once again you can't deny that it was also turning you

on. And just so you know it wasn't just the men who were enjoying the video, I was there in the office with all of the girls and I could tell you that most of them had pretty big smiles on their faces."

"Really, you think so?"

"Absolutely, didn't you notice yourself?"

"Sort of, but I will remind you that I was somewhat preoccupied with, you know, trying not to piss myself!"

"I'm just saying Jill that a lot of men and women both were getting a really hot and bothered by seeing you doing that little shimmy that you were doing in your very skimpy teeny tiny black bikini."

"Okay now you're just trying to make me feel really awkward about the whole thing more than I already am."

"Is it working?"

"I think that you know very well that it is!"

"Glad I could put those thoughts in your head, I'll see you at work tomorrow, have fun!"

The video chat ended as Jill sat there in her computer chair staring at the screen and looking at the number of likes that her video continued to gain by the moment. She had no doubt that the only reason the video was so popular was because she was dancing around like a crazy person trying to avoid peeing herself. And she could see from reading the comments, even though she knew you should never read the comments on an Internet board, that most of the people weren't fooled, they knew full well what she was doing, with there being a million comments about looking at that crazy girl doing that pee dance, and with many people mentioning they wished that she had left a wet spot on that bikini.

Jill stood up from her computer chair and looked around and saw that no one was nearby, and that was when she started stripping out of her clothes to change into her pajamas. But as she stood there naked she couldn't help but feel a tingling across her flesh. Something about it felt really exciting, even if nobody else could see her on the other side of the computer. But just the fact that she was looking at the video with its likes gathering by the minute while she was standing there naked started getting her excited.

It didn't take her long to get into bed and she decided that she would sleep naked that night, and she masturbated furiously until she fell into a deep sleep.

That night Jill had one of those dreams that she hadn't had in a while. She found herself going to work and was waving to all of her coworkers who all were smiling and waving back at her, and she couldn't help but notice that some of them were laughing.

"What's so funny?" Jill said as she stood there smiling with her hands on her hips confidently.

"Jill's naked!" Samantha said as she pointed at Jill.

"Very funny Samantha, you know very well that I'm not n-" Jill said as suddenly she started feeling her body and looked down and saw she was naked and then began screaming and covering herself up.

"Hey everybody, Jill's naked!" Kim shouted as everyone began laughing and clapping.

"Don't look at me!" Jill said as she ran behind the potted plant. But then Smithy, the janitor came and moved the plant away with a big smile and a thumbs-up as he started humming the tune to we wish you a Merry Christmas, which he seemed to know pretty well despite the fact that he was Jewish.

"Well Jill I can see that you dressed appropriately for work today," Kate said as she came over. "Are you ready to go over to the warehouse where you won't be able to go to the bathroom all day?"

"Wait, I need to find some clothing to put on!"

Kate shook her head. "No no Jill, you are wearing exactly the right thing, everybody liked you so much in that bikini that we thought we would show them a little more today, in fact from now on no more clothing at work for you!"

"What, you can't do that!" Jill said as she screeched in horror.

"Oh but I can, you signed a contract!" Kate said as she held up the contract and laughed evilly. "It said that you agreed to work in the warehouse without clothing and without bathrooms until the end of time and to do it on video!"

"No!" Jill shouted as she realized that all the video cameras were pointed at her and all of her coworkers were smiling and pointing at her and laughing.

"Smile Jill, you're naked on camera!" Kate laughed maniacally as she held up the contract, which Jill grabbed out of her hands and tried to use it to cover up her pubic area as she stood there blushing, while everyone continued pointing and laughing.

"No!" Jill shouted as she bolted up in bed. She looked around to see that no one was in the room except for her cat, who was staring at her and wondering what was wrong. "Oh, it was just a dream, a really titillating dream." Jill stood up and got out of bed and as soon as she did that she realized that her bladder was ready to explode, so she quickly bolted to the bathroom while dodging the cat and was glad she didn't have anything to pull down and was able to sit right on the toilet and began peeing loudly.

"That's the last time I go to bed naked," Jill said as she put on her pajamas and got back into bed.

The next morning Jill woke up and did her daily morning routine, making sure not to imbibe too many liquids as she finished up her breakfast and fed the cat. She got dressed in some of her more conservative clothing that didn't show as much skin, because after yesterday, to say nothing of the dreams that were provoked for her last night, she was feeling more self-conscious than usual.

"Well I see you're all dressed up today Jill," Leah said as she got in the car.

"I like the bikini better," Henry said as he laughed.

"So did the entire office, I just wish I wasn't driving the truck at the time," Ashley said.

"But I guess you saw the video, didn't you?" Jill said.

"Yeah, I saw it once or twice or 20 times and shared it with all of my friends and everybody that I knew," Ashley said as she burst out laughing.

"But it's not funny!" Jill shouted.

"No, of course not, it's hilarious!" Ashley said as everyone continued laughing.

Patricia shook her head and made some tsk tsk tsk noises. "You know Jill this is one of those other type of situations you could have avoided if you had better bladder control. Honestly yesterday you were going out of control like you were some type of chimp with itching powder in their panties."

"I had to pee dammit!" Jill said. "Like most people I can't get through the day without a bathroom, and having to model a bikini while your bladder is ready to explode isn't the easiest task in the world. Maybe you should try that sometime."

"I wonder what we have in store for work for us today," Henry said. "Maybe they will have everybody get naked this time!"

"Naked?" Jill said as she slumped down in the backseat and couldn't help but blush.

"Are you blushing at the mention of naked Jill?" Leah said with a smirk. Leah of course didn't know about the dream that Jill had had last night; it was more like an erotic nightmare, extremely terrifying but also exciting at the same time.

"Well I know I certainly didn't sign a contract for that," Jill said shaking her head.

"But you did sign a contract agreeing to work in a place that had no bathroom," Patricia said as she high-fived Leah.

"Well hey, at least you are making better money," Ashley said. "I know you may not think so, but they really do take care of their employees at this place, and I think that they are being quite generous with you."

"Well we can't all be lottery winners," Jill said as she rolled her eyes at Leah.

"Are you still going on about that," Leah said as she shook her head. "I just took 10 minutes to buy a lottery ticket, it's not like you were going to wet yourself because of that."

"Too bad," Ashley said as they all began laughing again.

The rest of the ride was uneventful and soon they were at work. As Jill walked towards all of her coworkers she couldn't help but notice that everybody was staring at her, and she pretty much knew why. While they were looking at her they were probably all picturing her in that little black bikini jumping up and down and crossing her legs furiously trying not to piss herself.

"Hi Jill," Kim said with a smile. "Not wearing the bikini today?"

"Is that suddenly going to be the standard uniform," Jill said shaking her head. "No, as far as I know that that's going to just be a one-time thing."

"Hey Jill, do you think I can talk to you for a moment," Kate said as she motioned for Jill to go over to her. "We seem to have been selling a lot of those bikinis that you were modeling yesterday and I was thinking that we have a whole variety of bikinis, and well we were wondering if maybe you would think about modeling them again today, you know for a little bit of a bonus as well?"

"Well I don't know," Jill said feeling genuinely conflicted about the whole situation.

"Well if you don't want it I suppose I could always offer the bonus to someone else," Kate said as she shook her head.

"Hey I didn't say no yet," Jill said shaking her head.

"So is that a yes then?"

Jill reluctantly nodded. "I guess so, but I draw the line at any type of thong. When I was in high school this guy who was harassing me teased me and he got everyone in the school to call me thong girl!"

Kate couldn't help but laugh. "I'm sorry, I just found that kind of funny."

"Yes so did my classmates," Jill said as she stuck out her tongue before bringing it right back into her mouth, not wanting to appear childish and immature in front of her boss.

"Anyway Jill here, go get changed into your new work uniform for the day," Kate said as she handed Jill a yellow bikini with pink polka dots on it. "This one is ridiculously feminine and girly but I think that you will look really nice in it, in that itsy-bitsy teeny-weeny yellow polka dot bikini. Hey we can even play that song while you are modeling the bikini and that will probably make it even more popular."

"You can't be serious," Jill said but she could tell from looking at Kate's eyes that she was dead serious. "But just give me a minute, I'll go get changed."

As Jill went into the bathroom to get changed she couldn't help but notice the irony of the fact that she dressed in a way that would hopefully be less revealing after what had happened yesterday, and now she was immediately getting changed into yet another skimpy little bikini that she would never normally be caught wearing in public. She really hoped that the new DVD planner she planned on buying that weekend was worth everything that she was putting herself through. Now she would probably buy the Deluxe Edition that also had a Blu-ray player, because why the hell not? She figured she earned it.

As Jill came out of the bathroom in her new bikini everyone in the office started whistling and hollering at her.

"I thought you said it was just going to be a one-time thing," Kim said with a big smirk as she laughed.

"Oh shut up," Jill said as she shook her head.

Kate drove Jill down to the warehouse where now she was doing double time. Not only was she modeling the bikini when she had downtime on the live video feed as a way of promoting the product, but she also had to go around the warehouse checking the inventory for everyone like she always had to.

Just like every day by the midday point, her bladder was becoming noticeably full. She knew that even though she was giving her bladder as much of a break as possible when she wasn't at work, and even though she was limiting her liquids throughout the day as much as possible without getting dehydrated in the warm stuffiness of the and air-conditioned warehouse, she still always had to go.

"I'll be right back in just a minute," Leah said as she stood up on videoconference.

"Wait, where are you going?" Jill said.

"Where do you think I'm going," Leah said as she looked towards the bathroom door.

"Do you really have to?"

"Yeah, do you really have to," Patricia added as she shook her head in disapproval at the idea of Leah using the bathroom at work.

Leah shrugged her shoulders. "It's not an emergency, but I figure why push things if I don't have to?"

"In solidarity with your fellow coworker, Jill, we're women, we go to the bathroom together, or in this case we should not go to the bathroom together."

"I feel like it's not healthy to hold it all day long, so if you'll excuse me I will just be using the little girl's room for a moment and then I will be right back," Leah said.

"I don't know what has gotten into her," Patricia said shaking her head many times. "Just thinking about all the germs crawling around on that toilet seat, it's enough to give a girl nightmares."

"There are a lot of things that could give a girl nightmares," Jill said as she once again suddenly felt herself feeling self-conscious as she thought of the dream that she had where she was at work naked. The fact that she was now feeling that she was nearly naked in that skimpy little bikini again, she knew wasn't going to make her nightmares go away, and they would probably only increase. At least this time she didn't have to get changed with the janitor watching behind a bunch of boxes.

As Leah sat on the toilet and relieved herself she had to admit that there was something that felt fiendishly evil about it. As she sat there releasing the contents of her bladder into the toilet loudly and proudly she couldn't help but think of poor Jill, sitting there in her skinny little bikini, her bladder filling by the moment. For some reason the fact that she knew Jill couldn't go to the bathroom was making the fact that she was going to the bathroom more enjoyable, titillating even.

"No, I'm doing this for my health, not for Jill," Leah said not wanting to admit to some degree that she was feeling spiteful towards Jill, not in a mean or unfriendly way, but something about the fact that it seemed like Jill was finally learning a lesson. If Jill didn't get to go to the bathroom at work she figured that somebody might as well.

"Did you say something about Jill," Samantha said. "You're not trying to torture her again are you?"

"I have never tortured Jill before, torture is against the Geneva Convention," Leah said.

"Do they have anything in the Geneva Convention about torturing someone's full bladder?" Samantha asked.

"I'm no expert on international law, but as far as I know it doesn't," Leah said. "So I think that even if I did torture Jill's bladder simply by relieving myself that I am fully in the clear, legally speaking."

Leah flushed the toilet and came out and washed her hands. She kind of wished that Jill could see all of that running water; she knew that it would drive Jill absolutely frantic. Maybe she really was a bit vindictive, about what she didn't know, but something about this new power she had as a result of the fact that she could use the bathroom and Jill could not, was sort of a nice feeling for her. It was intimate in sort of an evil way, if that made sense, which she knew it really didn't, but on some level it did.

Leah finally left the bathroom and she and Samantha both sat down where they saw Jill was already squirming in her bikini trying not to do a repeat of yesterday.

"Did you ladies have a good time chatting it up in the bathroom," Jill said as she stuck out her tongue.

Samantha and Leah looked at each other but didn't say anything, although Jill could detect something was going on between them, although what exactly she wasn't quite certain.

"Hey Jill do you think that you could see if we have any of those blue bikinis with the pink flowers on them in stock," Kim said. "It's okay, you don't have to wear them, and the one you are wearing right now is already skimpy enough for your many adoring fans."

"Let me check," Jill said as she stuck out her tongue and went over to the inventory and managed to find the blue bikini that Kim was looking for. She brought it over to the video and held it up. "Is this the one you wanted?"

Kim nodded. "I bet you would probably look great in that one as well Jill."

Jill continued working, and as usual as she walked around checking the inventory she could feel her bladder slowly filling up. She was trying to be more conscious of her movements so that she wouldn't embarrass herself like she did yesterday, but she couldn't deny the fact that her bladder was feeling exceptionally full as the day went on, and she couldn't help but cross and uncross her legs.

She was never an exhibitionist, but she had to admit that while she was doing this, or between doing her work, she would occasionally bring up on the computer her video and check the number of likes. So far it had been liked and shared over 1000 times, several thousand in fact. The idea that so many strangers suddenly knew who she was and knew her intimately was both titillating and making her feel more self-conscious by the minute.

"Hey Jill do you think you could bend over and get that piece of inventory that fell on the floor," Kim said as Jill slowly bent over and tried to pick up some snorkels and facemasks. Kim couldn't help but stare Jill right in the ass. She hadn't noticed before but Jill had a really nice ass, and seeing it sort of wiggling around with desperation put a smile on her face.

"Okay, I got everything," Jill said as she sat back down. But as soon as she sat back down it seemed like every few seconds Kim had another request to the point where Jill was constantly getting up and down, and every time she did that it put more pressure on her poor achingly full bladder.

No way could she be getting this many orders that fast. She almost felt like confronting her about it, but she thought that confronting her about what she thought was going on was even more awkward than what was going on. She knew that clearly Kim was manipulating her to make her as uncomfortable as possible, and it was definitely working.

By hour five she was firmly convinced that Kim had something of a closet sadist in her. She tried to dismiss these concerns, but then Kim finally put the nail in the coffin of any type of doubt that was in Jill's mind.

While Jill was standing there with her legs crossed modeling the bikini that was when she saw Kim moving towards the bathroom, but the curious thing was that she was bringing her laptop with her.

"What the hell?" Jill asked as Kim went into the bathroom, sat down on the toilet and started peeing very loudly.

"Is something the matter Jill?" Kim said with a big smile on her face.

"Did you just bring your laptop into the bathroom?" Jill asked, the sound of Kim peeing so loudly driving her absolutely out of her mind.

Kim laughed and shrugged her shoulders. "I guess I did, silly me."

Jill wanted to ask her why was she being so innocent, it was obvious that she did that on purpose, but again she didn't want to escalate the awkwardness of the situation and just wanted it to be over as soon as possible. So she finally settled on something less controversial. "Do you really think it's professional to bring your laptop into the bathroom with you?"

Kim laughed and shrugged his shoulders once again. "Well hey no one can accuse me of leaving my workstation and being derelict in my duty, and speaking of duty, no I'm just kidding, I'm totally done!"

Kim flushed the toilet and the loud flushing of the toilet made Jill practically want to cry.

"So where were we, oh yeah I need you to get the following items," Kim said as she started listing things, which Jill, being a diligent little worker bee, went around and got every last one of them, leaving her barely any time to sit and relax.

"Okay everybody, the work day is over," Kate said.

Jill was relieved, or at least she was closer to relief anyway, and it couldn't come soon enough.

As Kate came and picked up Jill, she told her what a great job she did and how great she looked in that little itsy-bitsy teeny-weeny yellow polka dot bikini that she wore to work that day. And she knew that she would never be able to get that song out of her head now.

In fact it was compounded because on the ride home all of her friends couldn't help but burst into a raging course of that song, claiming that it made things catchy and it made work more upbeat.

But as Jill ran out of the car and ran to her toilet and started peeing, she still couldn't get that thought out of her head, she couldn't deny it now, not only were people enjoying her being desperate, but she had a full-blown bathroom bully, and she didn't know exactly how she was going to deal with it.

9

Jill had to admit she didn't know exactly how to respond to the situation of having a bathroom bully. What do you do when an adult is bullying you? She tried to think back to everything in high school and she wasn't really good at dealing with bullies back then.

That was when she suddenly flashed back to something that had happened to her back in high school. It seemed so long ago, but she could still remember it really vividly, maybe because she could remember every instance in which she was desperate for a bathroom and was unable to use one.

Jill was walking down the hallway at school desperately in need of a bathroom but that's when she saw the bitchy girl from school, Jenny Sanderson, go into the bathroom.

"I don't want to go to the bathroom with Jenny in there!" Jill said but she could see that she was clearly crossing her legs. She had to go and she had to go pretty bad, but she thought that maybe she could wait another period before going to the bathroom.

As Jill sat in her next class all she could think about was how badly she had to pee. She was looking at the clock every few minutes and she even thought about asking the teacher to go to the bathroom, but she was too embarrassed to ask and thought that the teacher would probably say no, so why should she put herself through the embarrassment of asking when the answer was already pretty much a given?

She also couldn't help but notice that Jenny was sitting at the back of the class with a big smile on her face. It was totally unfair that she got to go to the bathroom while Jill didn't. Jill felt that she should stand up to Jenny, but she was not one for confrontation.

As soon as the bell rung she was eager to get to the bathroom as she knew she couldn't wait another period. Unfortunately as she was heading towards the bathroom she saw Jenny and her friends already heading towards the bathroom.

"No no no!" Jill said, practically ready to piss herself. She considered not going to the bathroom, but as she could feel the pressure in her bladder driving her crazy she knew that there was absolutely nothing she could do, she had to go and she had to go now!

Jill went into the bathroom and she saw that all of the stalls seemed to be taken. Standing in front of the stalls was Jenny.

"What are you doing here?" Jenny asked.

"It's a bathroom, take a guess!" Jill said certainly not wanting to pick a fight with Jenny but the pressure in her bladder wasn't giving her much of a choice.

Jenny knocked on the stall door. "Hey everybody Jill really needs to use the bathroom, so don't like take your time or anything."

"Please Jenny I have to go really bad!" Jill said as she put her hand up in an act of submission.

"It depends, what are you going to do for me?" Jenny asked.

"Just let me use the bathroom!" Jill shouted.

"You didn't say pretty please."

"Pretty please let me use the bathroom!" Jill said practically hopping from foot to foot.

"Sure you can use the bathroom, as soon as everyone else is done," Jenny said. "We certainly wouldn't want everyone to take an excessive amount of time."

Jill knew that Jenny was toying with her. The very fact that she was saying that was a signal to her friends inside of the stalls not to come out until after the bell rung, and they knew that Jill would never willingly be late to class. The sound of all those girls peeing loudly was driving Jill out of her mind.

Suddenly Jill heard all of the toilets flushing and for a moment she began to get hopeful. But then when all of the toilets stopped flushing they started flushing again.

"What are you doing in there?!" Jill shouted now actively dancing in front of the doors.

"Well we certainly wouldn't want them to not flush enough," Jenny said. "Listen to the sound of all those toilets flushing, isn't it beautiful, all those whooshing gushing sounds!"

Jenny then walked over to the sinks and started turning all of them on with the water hissing loudly.

"It looks like it's almost time for class, you don't want to be late, now do you Jill?!" Jenny said with an evil smile.

"Dammit!" Jill shouted as she ran out of the bathroom and made it to class just in the nick of time.

The next class was purely torturous and from the back of the class Jill could see Jenny with a big smile on her face. But the second the bell rung Jill made sure that she bolted for the bathroom and luckily managed to get to the bathroom before Jenny and her friends.

Of course when Jill came out of the stall Jenny and her friends were waiting there just the same and not saying anything, but Jill did not want to challenge their supremacy of the girls bathroom, so she simply washed her hands and got out of there, slinking away with her tail between her legs.

As Jill finished remembering her high school experience she shook her head. "No way am I going to let that happen to me ever again!"

At the same time though she didn't know exactly how to confront Kim or any of her other coworkers on the fact that they all seemed to be taking a lot of joy in her agonizing bladder pain.

"A bathroom bully?" Leah said on videoconference later that night. "You know Jill I have never accused you of being paranoid before but now I think that you are seeing things where they don't exist."

"But did you see how Kim was treating me yesterday; she was purposely keeping me constantly on the move so that she could watch me squirm!" Jill said.

Leah shook her head. "I don't think that you can prove that Kim was bullying you simply because you had to go to the bathroom. Yesterday was just a really busy day and there was lots of inventory to be had. Next you're probably going to accuse me of bullying you in the bathroom simply because I used the bathroom at work."

Jill had to admit that it was true, she was thinking that, but she didn't really want to admit it to Leah, and at the same time though she couldn't keep quiet on it. "Well yeah, sort of," she said.

"Jill I simply had to use the bathroom, just because someone uses the bathroom doesn't mean that they are being a bully."

"But you never had to use the bathroom at work before or anywhere else away from home, what gives?"

"I simply thought that maybe it would be healthier to go to the bathroom. You probably shouldn't hold it in all day."

"In case I have to remind you I do hold it all day, and I need it a lot more than you do!"

"How can you objectively say who needs to go to the bathroom more?"

"Well if you didn't go to the bathroom all day at work would you be able to make it without feeling a tremendous amount of pain?"

"I would be uncomfortable by the end of the day but certainly nothing that I couldn't handle."

"I spent nearly half the day in a state of near desperation and by the end of the day I am practically going out of my mind. And I don't think that Patricia approves of you going to the bathroom."

"But she doesn't approve of anyone going to the bathroom, anywhere, ever, under any circumstances."

"So are you going to the bathroom sort of as an affront to her rather than to me?"

Leah laughed. "Jill I'm not going to the bathroom as an affront to anyone, I'm going to the bathroom simply because I feel the need to use the bathroom and realize that it's probably not healthy to hold it all day."

"Exactly, which is why I should have a bathroom!"

Leah had to admit that she was getting excited watching Jill get all agitated over the fact that she didn't have a bathroom all day long. Leah didn't want to admit it to Jill, although she wasn't sure how well she was hiding it, she actually was quite enjoying the fact that Jill had to go to the bathroom all day and couldn't while she could. She had to admit to herself at least that partially the reason why she was going to the bathroom was simply because she knew that Jill couldn't. She knew that Patricia probably wouldn't approve, but she felt like she was rebelling against her as well, and her strict bladder regime. Going to the bathroom whenever she wanted without fearing the judgment of others was making her feel a new sense of freedom and liberation.

"Well it wouldn't be practical to give you a bathroom Jill, so I'm afraid you're just going to have to keep holding it."

"But you admit that it's unfair that I should have to hold it all day and probably not good for my health."

"Maybe Jill, but it still not practical to give you a bathroom, so I guess we'll just have to deal with it in our own way."

"What do you have to deal with? You don't have to go without a bathroom all day; you just get to watch me squirm all day!"

Leah laughed. "You know what Jill, I suppose you're right, lucky me, sucks for you. See you tomorrow!"

As Leah ended the call Jill let out a loud ear piercing scream that caused her cat to go running across the room.

"Sorry I didn't mean to scare you," she shouted to her cat but she had to admit that she had to get that all out. Sometimes when you are so frustrated you just have to let out a good scream to get it out of your system.

Now that Leah was off of the videoconference Jill decided that she would check her video again to see that the likes just continued going up, and that the video that she shot yesterday of her modeling the other bikini was doing likewise quite well. As she watched her video and the motions she couldn't help but notice that she was very obviously desperate, but she thought she did better on the second day of concealing it compared to the first day.

Jill got changed out of her clothing and she looked at the bikini that she had on her bed. Slowly but surely she put it on and started walking around the room. She had to admit that she still did feel practically naked wearing that bikini, but something about that was in and of itself kind of freeing. While Leah was discovering the freedom of being able to go to the bathroom whenever she wanted, Jill understood the freedom of being able to wear a bikini, even a very skimpy teeny weenie itsy-bitsy one.

It didn't take long for her to fall down on her bed and began masturbating to thoughts of her day. Her situation at work was infuriating, but the fact that she could masturbate to it at the end of the day at least made it something of a bit of a trade-off. Sure she would like to find some way out of the situation if she could possibly do so, but she didn't really see any way out of it, so she figured that she would just have to cope as best that she could, and this was one way in which she coped with it.

"A bathroom bully, now I've heard everything from you Jill," Ashley said on the ride to work the next day. "Besides if anyone is a bathroom bully it's you."

"How am I a bathroom bully, I am the one who doesn't have

access to a bathroom!" Jill said as she pointed to herself. "In order to be the one bullying people you have to be the one with the bathroom, the one with the power."

"Jesus Jill just because someone has access to a bathroom when you don't doesn't mean that it is some type of power play on their part," Patricia said shaking her head. "You are letting this bathroom situation drive you completely crazy. If anything you should willingly embrace this as an excellent opportunity to increase your bladder capacity and holding skills."

"Look I don't mind holding occasionally recreationally, but holding every day while I am trying to work makes my job extremely difficult," Jill said. "And the fact that everyone's being really mean to me about it doesn't help."

"Hey you were really mean to me when I wasn't able to use the bathroom when I was driving the truck," Ashley said.

"She's right Jill," Henry said.

"Sure take her side, you just are saying that because you're going to enjoy masturbating to thoughts of me without a bathroom all day," Jill said as she stuck out her tongue.

"Guilty as charged, but is that really a crime technically?" Henry said. "As far as I know we don't yet have a thought police that goes around patrolling our thoughts and arresting us based on the fact that we were having attractive thoughts from our coworker not being able to sit still because of her full bladder while wearing a really skimpy bikini. And I know you're going to say this is sexist somehow, but I don't care."

"Well it definitely is, but I suppose I can't blame you," Jill said. "I realize that situation reversed I can and have been a bit of a bitch about it, but this isn't even comparable to what I did to you Ashley. Sure I teased you occasionally while you were driving the truck, but you always got to a bathroom at some point during the day, even if you had to wait a long time for it. I have to go the whole day without any even possibility of using a bathroom. Do you have any idea how maddening that is?!"

"Yes, I kind of do Jill," Ashley said. "When you are trying to drive a truck and your friend is teasing you about the fact that you don't have a bathroom it certainly doesn't make their job any easier."

"Okay I admit that I did wrong, but two wrongs don't make a right. The fact that I occasionally teased you while you were driving the truck doesn't mean that I deserve my current fate. The fact is I am being bathroom bullied by Kim and our other coworkers."

"Maybe Kim has a crush on you," Leah said.

"No way," Jill said shaking her head.

"Well they do say that you tease the ones that you love," Leah said.

"That's what they say when boys tease girls and it only normalizes the behavior," Jill said. "But do you really think that Kim has a crush on me?"

Leah shrugged her head. "I don't know Jill, but I did enjoy the fact that I put that thought in your head, so have fun at work today when you are working with Kim!"

"Gee thanks a lot!" Jill said as she stuck out her tongue. But Leah was right, now that the thought had been put in her head she couldn't get that thought out of her mind, and all she could think about was what she was going to say to Kim when she got to work.

"Hey Jill," Kim said as she came over to Jill while she walked in to the office.

"Kim, hi!" Jill said not able to disguise the fact that she was feeling nervous. "How are you today?"

"I'm doing really well Jill; do you think you're going to be wearing any interesting bikinis today?" Kim said as she elbowed Jill in what she thought was a flirtatious manner, although maybe she was only thinking that because of what Leah was saying, and she didn't know exactly how to react now.

"As you can see I tried to dress a little bit more conservatively today," Jill said.

"Jill I am absolutely pleased with the work you have been doing here lately," Kate came over with a big beaming smile on her face. "The last two days where you have been modeling the bikinis have seen our sales go through the roof."

"No, don't tell me," Jill said.

Kate smiled. "Well we do have a really nice new bikini here today Jill and I think that it will look really great on you. It's that attractive blue one that I think you have probably seen in inventory. I will of course keep giving you a bonus as your popularity goes up."

"I thought I was a warehouse inventory worker, what am I now, a part-time bikini model?"

Kate rubbed her chin and shrugged her shoulders. "You know Jill I never actually thought about this as in where it fits in your job, but all I know is that your videos of you in those bikinis are going viral and we are getting more requests for them than we ever have before. I know I can't force you to do it or anything like that but —"

"Okay okay, I'll do it," Jill said shaking her head. "You don't have to twist my arm around over it. But I am hoping that this is a really good bonus I am getting for doing all of this."

"But trust me Jill you will not regret this," Kate said. "Now why don't you go get changed and I will bring you down to the warehouse."

Jill went into the bathroom to go get changed and that was when she heard someone else enter the room.

"Are you in here Jill?" Kim asked.

"Yeah I am," Jill said as she stood there naked in the stall, suddenly feeling self-conscious despite the fact that she knew that Kim couldn't see anything at the moment. "I'm getting changed."

"And going to the bathroom one final time before your long day at the warehouse," Kim said, and if Jill could see her she would realize that Kim was smirking and trying not to giggle.

Jill felt weird having a conversation where she was completely naked, even if the other person couldn't see her, so she quickly got dressed in the bikini, went to the bathroom and came out. While she was doing all of that she couldn't help but notice that Kim was in the stall right next to her. Jill almost felt like peeking into the stall because she could have sworn that Kim was breathing heavily and possibly even masturbating.

But Jill was not one for confrontation, so she quickly washed her hands and got out of the bathroom so that Kate could bring her to the warehouse.

Once Jill got to the warehouse it was pretty much business as usual. Fortunately in the early parts of the day things were easier because she didn't yet have to go to the bathroom, and she tried to limit her liquid intake as much as possible to make that stretch of time last as long as possible. However by hour three and four it was becoming once again obvious that she had to go to the bathroom.

Although Jill didn't want to say it, it was obvious that Kim was making her get up seemingly a lot more than was probably necessary, and every time that Kim saw her she had a big smile on her face. Jill couldn't help but think that maybe Leah was right, maybe Kim did have some type of a crush on her.

Eventually Kim got up to go to the bathroom, and that was when Jill's curiosity got the better of her.

Leah I think you might be right, Jill said to Leah in a private text message and went on to say how she thinks that Kim was falling in love with her and maybe she could find out if that was the case.

"What are we sixth-graders," Leah said out loud before she texted that to Jill, before adding though I am glad that I got the thought in your head and you can't get it out of there.

Jill had to admit it was one of those situations where you weren't supposed to think about the elephant. When a person told you not to think about the elephant it was all you could think about. And right now all Jill could think about was the fact that Kim was totally lezing out on her and she didn't know exactly how to respond to such a situation. Actually that wasn't the only thing that she could think about, she was also thinking about her growing need to pee and how it was getting worse with each passing moment.

That was when Leah stood up.

"Where are you going, don't tell me," Jill said as she shook her head.

"Hey if you want me to get the skinny on Kim I have to talk to her don't I," Leah said as she got up and started heading towards the bathroom.

Jill wasn't sure if she should be grateful to Leah for going to the bathroom to potentially spy on Kim, or just infuriated over the fact that they were both going to the bathroom while she was sitting there with her bladder rapidly filling and her legs tightly crossed, which was much more obvious when all you were wearing was a really tiny bikini.

Leah walked into the bathroom and went to approach a stall and push the door open and when she did she saw Kim there with her pants down rubbing herself between the legs.

"Oh Kim, Jesus Christ I am sorry!" Leah said as she closed the door feeling really awkward over the fact that she caught Kim in an act of office masturbation. She had to admit it made her feel really uncomfortable, but at the same time it kind of vindicated her because it showed that her theory was right, Kim did seem to be masturbating to the fact that Jill was unable to use the bathroom.

But then she remembered the reason she was there in the first place, went into the stall next to Kim and began going to the bathroom. As she finished up going to the bathroom she had to admit that the whole situation was making her excited as well, so she very slowly started masturbating to the thought that right now Jill was there in her bikini in agonizing bladder pain. She almost pictured herself in Jill's situation, and something about the fact that she was now getting to go to the bathroom as well as masturbate while Jill was sitting there with all that pressure inside of her trying to control herself was making her feel powerful. Maybe Jill was right, maybe it was indeed a power play.

"What is wrong with me," Leah said as she came out of the bathroom and saw Kim at the sink. Neither of them said anything but she figured that there was an unspoken agreement that they both knew what both of them were doing and if both of them never said anything the secret would be safe.

"Well it's good to see you are both back," Jill said. "Have a good time?"

Leah and Kim sort of looked at each other awkwardly.

"Yeah, it's great being able to go to the bathroom whenever I want," Leah said. "But hey nothing unusual happened, right?"

"Of course not," Kim said, although Jill could tell that something was going on between them. She wasn't socially proficient enough to know exactly what, but she knew that something happened in the bathroom and now that was going to occupy her thoughts.

"You guys didn't miss anything, just Jill bending over in her bikini to get some more inventories," Samantha said with a smile. Now Jill was wondering if she was in on this whole thing. She couldn't help but notice that all of her coworkers once again seemed to be smiling, and once again she couldn't help but think that maybe they were in some type of global conspiracy against her to keep her in a state of desperation for everyone's entertainment. But maybe she wanted to believe that, because even though it would make her even more paranoid, at the same time it would keep things interesting, at the very least.

"Hey Jill I just delivered a whole bunch of those bikinis that you are modeling," Ashley said. "The guy I dropped them off with seemed a little bit creepy, because as far as I could tell he lived alone and it's weird when a single guy orders a bunch of female bikini bathing suits, but I think that we have you to thank for that. I think that you're probably going to be in his dreams tonight, and we know what type of dreams those will be, really wet ones!"

"Shut up!" Jill shouted. She felt like this probably violated office protocol in some way for a sexual tension free environment, but she wasn't about to say anything against her friends, even if they were taking advantage of the situation.

"He's not really a creep though, he was really nice, even let me use his bathroom," Ashley said with a snort.

"Okay now you're just trying to rub that in," Jill said and Kim and Leah couldn't help but look at each other at the mention of rubbing something in, rubbing one out was more like it, as they both thought of their experience in the bathroom together.

Ashley laughed and shrugged her shoulders and smiled. "Maybe," she said as she laughed even louder.

Jill continued to do her job but she couldn't help but notice that as time went on and she became more and more visibly desperate, that the demands on her got even more strenuous, and she couldn't help but think that all of her coworkers had it out for her today, had it out for her and her tiny little bladder.

By the end of the day Jill was eager to get changed once again and was glad for the opportunity to use the bathroom at work before she had to get in the car with everyone else.

On the way home from work they stopped for drinks since

Jill didn't have to rush home to get to the bathroom. But as she sat there next to Leah she couldn't help but notice that she was acting especially quiet and that she probably had a secret, but she was afraid to ask what.

After getting home from drinks Jill quickly went to the bathroom and thought that she should probably get changed for the night. At first she reached for her pajamas but then she shrugged her shoulders, reached for the bikini and decided that she was going to wear it to bed that night.

It would be a very long night.

10

Jill found that there wasn't all that much she could do about her situation. Every time she brought up the bathroom situation to Kate, Kate would just sort of dismiss it out of hand and point out the fact that she agreed to that when she signed her contract, even though she didn't feel that it was very fair, seeing as she didn't realize what she was signing at the time, although in the future she would probably be more careful about that.

She was enjoying the fact that she was getting larger paychecks and she was pretty happy with that new DVD player that she had, but she felt it was all taking a toll on her. Every day she would be modeling a new bikini and squirming in her seat, and by the time she got home her bladder was so sore and aching that she practically just wanted to go right to sleep.

"I don't know how much you can take bladder," Jill said as she massaged her bladder in the bathtub one night. "I realize I've been putting you through a lot lately. I have no idea how Patricia can go all day without a bathroom but I know that it's not easy for someone like me, and all of my coworkers seem to be taking advantage of the fact that they can go to the bathroom when I can't. Everyone seems to be against me, even Leah is peeing at work now and it's driving me crazy."

At the same time Jill couldn't deny that all of this bladder pain was also making her incredibly horny. As soon as she got home from work she couldn't help but masturbate like crazy. She knew that she hated the situation but at the same time it was making her so excited that it had her pretty much in a constant state of arousal. She would work all day with a full bladder and then come home and masturbate like crazy while wearing her bikini.

"This can't be healthy in the long run," Jill thought to herself now that she had been working at her job for a couple of weeks. She was in sort of a vicious cycle where she knew she couldn't get out of the situation and the situation was infuriating her, but at the same time it was getting her all hot and bothered, and it was practically all she could think about. But she thought that in the long term she was going to have to do something before she damaged her bladder.

"I just really think that this warehouse job might not have been the best idea," Jill said in the car the next day.
"I'm enjoying the extra money and everything but I don't know how much longer my bladder can take this! You know if I could switch back to the office with all of you guys I think that I would definitely do it."

"You'd be surprised at what you can get used to though Jill," Patricia said. "I have to admit that I have a newfound respect for you. You didn't think that you would ever be able to hold it all day at work and here you have been doing so for a couple of weeks now, you should be proud of yourself. You on the other hand Leah, you backslided, I don't know how you could possibly use a public toilet every day at work."

"It's not like I'm going constantly, I go once a day maybe, it's good to give the bladder a rest once in a while," Leah said.

"But when does my bladder ever get a rest?!" Jill shouted. "Sure I can hold it all day at work, but by the end of the day I am going completely and utterly out of my mind. All I can think about is getting to a bathroom by the end of the day."

"I have to admit it is kind of funny that Jill and Leah have basically switched places," Ashley said as she laughed. "It used to be that Leah would hold it all day without problem, and now she's going to the bathroom while Jill is the one who has to hold it all day."

"It's not funny!" Jill shouted. "And it's really not fair at all! Besides Leah used to choose to hold all day, I have no choice in the matter!"

"And now I choose to go to the bathroom during the day, so I don't put too much of a strain on my bladder," Leah said.

"I know but that's the difference, you have a choice, I have no choice!" Jill shouted.

"You chose to work in the warehouse," Ashley said. "You did sign a contract."

"But I didn't know that there wasn't going to be a bathroom and that by signing that I was pretty much waving my right to bathroom access," Jill said.

"I guess that will teach you to sign things without reading them more carefully," Leah said. "But all I know is that I find it a lot easier to get through the day with that mid-day pee."

"I would kill for a mid-day pee!" Jill shouted.

"Doesn't anyone appreciate the virtues of holding it in," Patricia said shaking her head. "I think that there is far too much urinary freedom in this society, they should get rid of all public bathrooms, and then people would be forced to hold it."

"At this point I would prefer that simply because then at least we would all be on equal playing ground," Jill said. "Not having a bathroom is worse by virtue of the fact that you do all have a bathroom, that's what you don't understand. So just because I signed a contract now I have to endure this as my fate forever?"

"Pretty much," Henry said as he laughed.

"It's not funny, I could be doing bladder damage," Jill said.

"No you are making your bladder stronger by not letting it dictate your life," Patricia said.

"It still does dictate my life!" Jill said shaking her head. "The fact that I can't go to the bathroom means I have to plan my entire day around that. I have to try to maneuver through the day with an increasingly full bladder while you can all casually sit back with empty bladders and enjoy watching me desperate."

"I won't lie Jill, this is pretty sweet," Ashley said. "I just wish I didn't have to drive the truck all day so that I could enjoy this even more. You are pretty much getting your just desserts."

"Okay so I made fun of you a few times while you had to go to the bathroom in the truck, I'm sorry, do I deserve to be punished until the end of time for that? That's the thing though too, I never get to see any of you guys desperate! Sure we all enjoy seeing women desperate for the bathroom, but when do I ever get to see you guys desperate, you get to see me every single day while having bathroom access the entire time."

"I have to admit it is incredibly entertaining," Henry said. "I don't mind holding myself sometimes but I have to admit that at work it is better to just be able to go to the bathroom."

Jill shook her head. "Once again you guys get a free show, getting to watch me squirm all day while getting to go to the bathroom, it's a double standard or something like that. That's what makes it even more frustrating, I would love to see others desperate, if only the situation were reversed once in a while, then at least it would be fair, like maybe if they rotated who was in the warehouse each day."

"Oh well, there's nothing you can do about it Jill, so I guess you'll just have to get used to it," Patricia said.

"Easy for you all to say!" Jill shouted shaking her head. "Well at least today we all have an office meeting, so I won't have to even go to the warehouse. It will be nice being able to go to the bathroom for a change and not have to be sitting around desperate in a skimpy little bikini."

"Well I'm sure that Kim will be disappointed about that," Leah said with a smirk.

Jill stuck out her tongue as they arrived at work.

At the office meeting they had lots of drinks passed around, and Jill felt nice to think that for a change she didn't have to watch her liquid intake because the bathroom was really only a few feet away. The meeting was actually kind of boring but the fact that Jill knew that they would get a bathroom break soon enough made it all worthwhile.

"And let's give a special round of applause for Jill who has helped us sell so many new bikinis lately," Kate said as everybody clapped.

Jill couldn't help but blush and waive sheepishly, as she still felt kind of awkward and embarrassed about the fact that all of her coworkers have seen her desperate and squirming around in that skimpy little bikini, in fact a whole bunch of different skimpy little bikinis. She couldn't help but notice that of all her coworkers Kim was still smiling the widest and kept looking at Jill.

Finally the meeting was over and people had time to mingle but Jill decided that she would go and use the bathroom simply because she relished the fact that she could.

"Are you in the bathroom Jill?" Kim said as she came into the bathroom.

"Yes, today I can actually use the bathroom," Jill said as she had a nice relaxing pee. "I have to admit this is a pretty nice bathroom that the office has. I wish they would install one of these in the warehouse."

"I guess it must be hard being in the warehouse all day," Kim said as she sat down in the stall next to Jill and began peeing loudly.

"But you don't know the half of it," Jill said as she finished going to the bathroom. She felt like maybe she should confront Kim about her bullying, but Jill was once again not one for confrontation.

"Well Jill I think that you're doing a great job and that you look great in all those bikinis that you are modeling, I would probably be far too self-conscious to model a bikini like that, especially on video where thousands of people can watch."

"Well hey it's worth the bonus, but trust me you wouldn't want to work in the warehouse all day without a bathroom."

"Tell me about it," Kim said as she finished using the bathroom as the two of them washed their hands at the sink.

As the two of them looked in the mirror that was when all of the sudden Kim leaned forward and kissed Jill on the lips. As soon as they did so the two of them backed off and looked at each other.

"What just happened here?" Jill said, shocked by what Kim had done.

"I'm sorry that was probably inappropriate!" Kim said suddenly red with embarrassment.

"No it was okay, I was just really surprised is all," Jill said as the two of them looked at each other before kissing again.

Just at that moment Leah walked into the bathroom with a look of shock on her face.

"Hey don't let me interrupt you," Leah said as she walked out of the bathroom with a big smile on her face muttering under her breath "knew it."

The two of them laughed and blushed once again.

"Hey Jill do you think you might like to get a drink sometime, like after work or something?" Kim asked with a smile.

"Actually my friends and I were thinking about going out for drinks after work today if you would like to come with us, I'm sure they wouldn't mind."

"Sure sounds great."

While Jill and Kim were getting to know each other in the biblical sense in the bathroom, Patricia was talking to Kate.

"I think that Jill is doing a really great job in the warehouse but I'm starting to think that maybe she would probably like to be in the office with everyone else, she keeps bringing up that whole bathroom thing," Kate said. "I was thinking of maybe we should rotate who is in the warehouse every day. I was also thinking that maybe we could have Kim work in the warehouse. I was wondering what you thought about that?"

Patricia tried not to smile too wide at the idea. She was thinking about the conversation she had had with Jill just a few hours before in the car, where she was practically begging for the possibility of getting out of her contract that condemned her to the bathroomless warehouse.

Patricia felt a momentary amount of guilt before shaking her head. "You know what I think that Jill's doing pretty good in the warehouse, and besides if she wasn't in the warehouse how would she model the bikinis every day?"

"I was also thinking about maybe promoting Kim since she has done such a good job, maybe making her Jill's supervisor in the warehouse, from the office of course," Kate said.

Now Patricia was practically on cloud nine. She knew that Kim was bullying Jill over the fact that she couldn't use the bathroom, and now she had the possibility of Kim being her supervisor.

Patricia nodded. "You know what I think that Kim would make an excellent supervisor for Jill."

"Great, you know I really value your input, and that's why I decided to ask you about this," Kate said. "So I guess we will keep Jill in the warehouse on a permanent basis and we will just keep everything as is."

"You know I think that sounds really really great," Patricia said trying hard not to be grinning from ear to ear. "I think that being in the warehouse has been really good for Jill."

Just then Jill came out of the bathroom and started walking over to Patricia as Kate left.

"Hey what were you just talking about with Kate?" Jill asked.

"Oh nothing important, just office stuff," Patricia said.

"Do you think it would be okay if Kim came and had some drinks with us after work?" Jill asked.

Patricia shrugged her shoulders. "Sure I don't see why not, we can celebrate Kim's promotion."

"Promotion?"

"Yeah Kate says that she was going to make Kim your supervisor."

"Great," Jill said as she suddenly thought of the possibility that now she would be constantly under Kim's control while her bladder was full, and the thought was both exciting and terrifying.

For the next couple of hours it was mostly a social atmosphere at the meeting where people were just mingling and having drinks, as it was basically for the rest of the day it was pretty much a recreational day.

"Well thank you everyone for an excellent meeting and you will all be returning to your regular jobs tomorrow," Kate said. "Meeting adjourned."

Kim agreed to meet them at the bar after work since she had her own car, but as Jill sat in the car with her friends and coworkers she knew that it would inevitably come up.

"So are we not going to talk about what happened in the bathroom today," Leah said.

"What do you mean?" Jill asked.

"Well I hate to say I told you so but –" Leah began saying with a smile.

"Okay so you were right about Kim, and you know I am glad about that, I just hope that it won't be anything awkward while we are having drinks tonight."

"Awkward over the fact that Kim is going to be your supervisor," Patricia said.

"Meaning that while you are working all day without a bathroom she will basically be in charge of you," Ashley said.

"Hey I wish it were the other way around, but hey what are you going to do," Jill said as she shrugged her shoulders.

"Well I'm glad that you have finally accepted things the way they are Jill," Patricia said.

"I wouldn't say that necessarily," Jill said shaking her head. "But I guess for now there's nothing I can do about it, it's not like I can get out of the situation."

Patricia tried not to smirk but once again she couldn't help it. "Of course not, you got yourself into this, so now you just have to deal with the consequences."

"And we will all enjoy dealing with the consequences as well," Leah said with a laugh that came across as arrogant and it was kind of making Jill aggravated.

"Well here we are," Henry said as they arrived at the bar.

They all got out of the car where they met up with Kim and walked in the door.

"Would you like me to buy you a drink Jill," Kim said with a fiendishly evil smile.

"Why are you smiling like that?" Jill asked.

"Well the really great thing about this bar is that the drinks are free tonight," Kim said as she looked at her watch. "We just have to wait another minute or so."

"Wait a minute, oh no not tonight," Jill said as she suddenly looked towards the bathroom and began walking towards it.

"Welcome everybody to our weekly bladder buster, everybody drinks free until the first person goes to the bathroom!" the bartender announced.

"What's the matter Jill; have to go to the bathroom?" Leah asked with a fiendish smirk.

Jill shrugged her shoulders. "Luckily I went to the bathroom at work today, although I did have a couple of drinks before I left, but it's nothing I can't handle. Maybe you have to go to the bathroom, you seem to have been doing a lot of that lately."

"Yeah I have definitely noticed," Patricia said. "You have been going to the bathroom at work pretty much every day now Leah."

"Yeah just once a day though," Leah said. "It's not like I have gone to excess or anything."

"It's once a day more than I get to go to the bathroom!" Jill said. "Something you haven't really been letting me forget. Ever since you started going to the bathroom at work you have been really cocky about it."

"What, it's my right to use the bathroom if I need to," Leah said. "If you wanted to go to the bathroom you shouldn't have been stupid enough to sign a contract saying that you would work in a building without any bathrooms."

"I think that you're going to the bathroom at work just to stick it to me," Jill said.

"Maybe I am, what are you going to do about it?" Leah said as she put her hands on her hips and smiled.

"You know I am thinking that maybe my bladder capacity is going up while yours is going down," Jill said as she put her hands on her hips and started walking around Leah.

"Hey I can still hold better than you can," Leah said. "In case you haven't forgotten I was always able to get through the day without going to the bathroom by choice, you just managed to get through the day by the skin of your teeth and can barely sit still. By the end of the day you're pretty much flopping around like a fish out of water desperately longing for a bathroom with hardly another thought in your mind."

"Holding contest!" Ashley said. "You two should have a holding contest, right here, right now."

"But it's the bladder buster," Jill said. "We don't want to have to go to the bathroom at the bladder buster."

"Well that will definitely encourage you to hold on," Patricia said. "And I think that you are right, I think that Leah is losing her bladder capacity while yours is building up Jill."

"I can out hold Jill easily," Leah said as she crossed her arms and shook her head.

"Well there's only one way to settle this," Kim said as she put down two large drinks in front of them. "Drink up you two!"

"What are the stakes?" Ashley said.

"If I win I think that you should stop going to the bathroom at work in solidarity with me," Jill said to Leah. "As I know you are totally just going to the bathroom to spite me."

"And when I win I think that I want you to go to a public place dressed in the bikini," Leah said.

"Fine," Jill said as she and Leah shook hands and started slowly drinking their drinks. Jill didn't even want to admit to Leah that under her clothing she was actually wearing the bikini that she had bought, because she had gotten so used to wearing a bikini every day at work that it felt kind of good to know that underneath her more conservative work clothing was her less conservative, well what would usually be her work clothing.

Two of them began slowly drinking their drinks, and in the beginning they were both relatively comfortable. They could feel the tension in the air, this was a standoff, a matter of principle, and all of their friends were enjoying watching every moment.

"Keep drinking you guys," Ashley said as she brought more tall glasses for them to drink.

"Are you sure that we should be drinking this much, I don't know if that's healthy," Jill said as she looked into her glass.

"What's the matter, don't think you can win?" Leah said as she began drinking.

"Not at all," Jill said as she drank more.

The two of them stared angrily at each other, neither one of them wanting to blink, and neither one of them wanting to admit that they both had to pee really badly. For the first hour they were okay but by then all of their friends could see that they were shifting in the legs a lot and looking more uncomfortable and less casual by the minute.

"So read any good books lately," Jill said trying to hide the fact that her legs were shaking.

"Plenty," Leah said as she sat there with her legs crossed as subtly as possible. Both of them were regretting the fact that they had a lot to drink before they left the office, and now it was all hitting them and hitting them hard.

"Well it looks like nobody ended the bladder buster yet, so I guess it's time to keep drinking," Ashley said as Jill and Leah groaned. "What's the matter, getting full?" Ashley pushed two large drinks in front of them.

Jill and Leah both took their glasses and started guzzling the drinks before slamming the glasses down on the table and staring at each other with angry glares. By now they were both shifting in their seats and their friends couldn't help but snicker and laugh. You could cut the tension in the room with a knife.

"Don't worry Jill, I think you can do it," Kim said as she patted Jill on the back causing Jill to cringe. "Sorry, I didn't mean to shake you up like that."

"How are you doing," Jill said crossing and uncrossing her legs constantly now.

"I'm doing just fine, how about you," Leah said, her legs shaking like crazy.

"Just peachy," Jill said as she gritted her teeth.

"Raindrops keep falling on my head," Henry started singing as the rest of them all started joining in.

"Shut up!" Jill and Leah both shouted loudly and simultaneously as everyone burst out laughing.

"Would you prefer don't go chasing waterfalls?" Ashley said as Leah and Jill snarled at her. "Okay okay, I get the message."

"I'm going to make you wear that bikini," Leah said.

"What, do you think that I care about the bikini," Jill said shaking her head.

"No way would you ever willingly wear a bikini in public like you did on that video," Leah said shaking her head.

"I'll show you what I wouldn't do," Jill said as she started undressing revealing herself to be wearing her skimpy bikini as everyone in the bar started whistling and hollering.

"Hey, it's the girl from the video!" someone said as they started snapping a picture with their phone.

"Well, this is hot," Kim said as Jill started blushing before she immediately sat down, crossed her legs tightly and put her hands between her legs.

"I really shouldn't have stood up like that," Jill said as she squirmed in her seat.

"I'll admit you have guts," Leah said as she crossed her legs tightly and put her hands between her legs as she and Jill stared at each other, both trembling and clearly about to go out of their ever loving minds.

"Well ladies and gentlemen the bladder buster has ended as somebody has used the bathroom," the bartender announced as a woman came out of the bathroom as everyone started booing her.

Jill and Leah looked at each other and they looked at the large group of people stampeding towards the bathroom as the line started rapidly building up.

"Well hey it looks like we can finally use the bathrooms," Ashley said as she looked at Leah and Jill before laughing. "Well most of us anyway."

Jill and Leah looked at each other and then they looked at the very rapidly growing bathroom line as their lips began trembling and their eyes began watering. They both sat there with their legs tightly crossed, their hands pressed between their legs, and their whole bodies trembling.

"Jill I'm sorry that I peed at work all the time, I was just doing it to annoy you," Leah said.

"I'm sorry I can't blame you for that, if I could go to the bathroom I definitely would have gone to the bathroom and done the exact same thing, I was foolish to sign that agreement to work in the warehouse," Jill said. "And I would definitely love seeing you without a bathroom all day in the warehouse, even though it wouldn't be as hard for you as it is for me."

"I totally realize that now Jill," Leah said as she looked at the rather sizable bathroom line that Ashley, Kim and Henry were all waiting in. "What would you say to a truce? The bladder buster has already ended and I think that we're both about ready to explode here."

"What are you saying, that you can't go on," Jill said smiling thinking that she was about to win this thing and see Leah admit defeat.

"Well if you want to continue the contest," Leah said as she tightly gripped her chair.

Jill and Leah looked at each other and then they looked at the bathroom line.

"Truce," Jill said as she extended her hand.

"Truce," Leah said as she shook Jill's hand. "The contest is over, now out of my way, I have to pee!"

"Me first!" Jill said as the two of them got on the end of a rather long line. Jill poked herself outside of the line and shook her head. "Does anyone think that maybe I can cut?"

All of the women in front of them in line looked and shook their heads and gave them angry glares.

"Well this is certainly humbling," Leah said as the two of them stood there with their legs tightly crossed bending at the knees and jogging in place.

"Wow it sure feels good to pee," Ashley said as she came out of the bathroom with a big smile on her face along with Henry, who used the men's room with pretty much no wait.

Jill and Leah snarled at their friends who just stood there laughing knowing that they wouldn't be able to get out of line to do anything to stop them.

Patricia stood shaking her head. "They really are animals, letting their bladders dictate their lives."

Patricia carefully looked both ways, carefully snuck out of the bar, looked both ways, went into the alley, squatted and began peeing very loudly before finishing up and smiling. "Well what they don't know won't hurt them!"

Patricia came back and saw her friends standing in line there.

"Where did you go?" Ashley said.

"I just stepped out for a moment," Patricia said smiling. "Honestly you are both letting your bladders rule your lives. If you just learn to hold it a little bit –"

"Shut up!" Jill and Leah both shouted at Patricia with snarls.

"Okay I'm shutting up," Patricia said before stepping a few paces away with the others as they burst into a rendition of don't go chasing waterfalls.

As Kim sat in the bathroom masturbating to the thoughts of all the women bursting outside of the restroom door, she couldn't help but think that maybe what she was doing was evil, but at that moment she didn't care, and she continued enjoying herself until finally someone started knocking on the door and shouting.

Eventually Jill and Leah were next in line and they were both practically sweating bullets at the fact that they had to go to the bathroom so bad.

"Please let me go first," Jill said. "Look, I'm even wearing the bikini and everything."

"Well Jill I suppose it's only fair that –" Leah said as the door opened, she pushed Jill out of the way and slammed the door shut.

"Leah open up in there!" Jill said as she tugged on the door knob and pounded on the door with her fist. "Hell hath no fury like a woman with a full bladder scorned!"

As Leah jerked down her panties and had a loud forceful pee she never felt so relaxed in all of her life, and she felt like she could practically go to sleep sitting on the toilet. Then she decided that she might as well start masturbating because the sound of Jill screaming outside of the bathroom was putting her in the mood. She knew that Jill would be angry, but she also knew that there was nothing that Jill could do about it right now, so for the next couple of minutes she was going to enjoy herself as much as possible.

"Leah!" Jill shouted at the top of her lungs outside the door until she could be heard echoing down the streets.

Epilogue

It was a nice sunny day on the beach and Jill was walking with her friends and enjoying the newfound freedom that came with being able to wear her bikini without feeling embarrassed.

As Jill walked arm in arm with Kim, she enjoyed the feeling of the sun on her mostly uncovered skin.

"This is just the type of thing I need after a long and busy week at work with my bladder," Jill said. "Because I have a really brutal supervisor."

"But I'm still your favorite," Kim said as she kissed Jill on the cheek causing her to blush and causing their friends to make all sorts of whistling and hollering noises.

"Sorry again that I took so long in the bathroom and then you ended up wetting yourself in public like that, and that the video went viral," Leah said.

Jill shrugged her shoulders. "Well it wasn't my proudest moment, but a bathing suit is meant to get wet I suppose. But don't you ever do that ever again!"

"Hey it's bikini dance girl!" a guy said as he snapped a picture of Jill as he went by and waved to which Jill simply waved back and shook her head.

"I'm just glad that now I can enjoy the beach and relax, and that if I have to go to the bathroom I can go whenever the hell I want!" Jill said as she walked up to the bathroom door turned the handle and found it locked. She simply shook her head and laughed. "Last one to the ocean —"

<u>Some Words from the Author</u>

I wrote this novel back in April 2020 and it took me around a year to getting around to reading and editing this in preparation for publishing it because I have a large backlog of things that I want to publish, both under my pseudonym through which I publish omorashi literature, as well as under my own name, so it took me a long time to get around to doing this but I think it's actually interesting from the standpoint of reading this back a year later.

I originally conceived of this novel when I was offered a job myself with an environmental group and didn't realize until after I had taken the job that it's a job that outdoors, often away from bathrooms with no bathroom access whatsoever. Obviously as soon as I realized that I began freaking out and panicking and everything like that. I was assured that lots of these places that I would go would most likely have some type of public restroom that I could use, so I managed to calm down a little bit.

However after I had accepted the job but before the job started that was when we started getting involved in the Covid pandemic and everything started shutting down, including lots of public bathrooms, public bathrooms that I would be relying on for the first time ever, so I was basically back in panic mode and the irony of the fact that I write omorashi literature, stories about women desperate for a bathroom or deprived of a bathroom, and was now finding myself in a situation where I was soon to be living things that I had previously only written about in fiction was quite intimidating, and I think that I ended up writing this book in order to try and cope with the idea of what that might be like, even though the situation in the book is actually completely different largely from my own experience at my outdoor job, the reality of which is a lot worse, but perhaps more realistic than the situations in this book that you have just finished reading and that I hope you enjoyed.

For one thing at no point during my environmental job was I ever asked to model a bikini on WebCam with a full bursting bladder! That was just something I thought of randomly while I was writing the novel and I think that it actually worked pretty well within the plot of the novel itself, and that to me that was probably one of the more unrealistic aspects of this novel, but hey you have to have some suspension of disbelief right?

Basically as soon as I figured out that I was going to be at a job potentially without bathrooms on a regular basis I started going back to talk to all of the people in the omorashi community that I had talked to over the years, some of whom I had actually made fun of over the fact that they were at jobs without bathrooms, so karma has a way of getting you back in getting you back bad, because not only now was I going to be at a job outdoors potentially without bathrooms, it just happened to be at the worst possible timing due to Covid because all the outdoor public bathrooms were closing, and a lot of those people that I had teased mercilessly about the fact that they didn't have a bathroom were now going to be working at home, with better bathroom access than before, putting me in the total opposite position for the first time ever.

Shortly after this happened I started to conduct a poll with another one of my omorashi friends (who the character of Patricia is based off of) who had told me that a woman should be able to hold it basically all day and that it should be no big deal. Obviously I disagree with her, I disagreed with her rather strongly, so we ended up making a poll about whether a woman should be inherently entitled to having bathroom access at a job in any and all circumstances. The exact wording of the poll was as follows:

Should Jill Have to Hold at Work?

Jill and Pgirl76 have just started a new job at an office. If Pgirl and Jill worked in an office but in different buildings far apart, where Pgirl and Jill's other coworkers had access to a bathroom whenever they needed it but Jill had to work in the warehouse, which lacks bathroom access because it would be cost prohibitive or impractical to construct one, and thus she has to go all day without one, would that be fair? Also Jill would be communicating with her coworkers, who have bathroom access, by video all day long.

1) No, it is unfair that Jill should have to go all day without bathroom access when her coworkers can go whenever they please and kind of cruel as well since she'd have to interact with them all day while they can use the bathroom and she cannot.

2) Yes, it is fair. If it is cost prohibitive and impractical to provide a bathroom in the warehouse and Jill is still willing to work the job she should have to put up with the fact that there is no bathroom and just learn to hold it in as part of the job. Not every job is 100% comfort and sometimes you just must deal with inconveniences like this.

We ended up setting the poll for one month and I felt pretty confident after the first day when most people were agreeing with my side, as I thought it was pretty much a given that anyone would agree that a bathroom is a basic thing that anyone should be able to have at work like that. However over the course of the month it was sort of a neck and neck race where every single day when we checked the poll, where it seemed like we were always ahead or behind by one single point changing on a daily day to day basis and everything like that, so it was turning into a real nail biter, especially towards the end, and it really was basically a photo finish more or less, or rather a screenshot finish I guess you would say in this case.

When we closed the poll exactly one month later the results were as follows:

1) No, it is unfair that Jill should have to go all day without bathroom access when her coworkers can go whenever they please and kind of cruel as well since she'd have to interact with them all day while they can use the bathroom and she cannot. 50% (127

votes)

2) Yes, it is fair. If it is cost prohibitive and impractical to provide a bathroom in the warehouse and Jill is still willing to work the job she should have to put up with the fact that there is no bathroom and just learn to hold it in as part of the job. Not every job is 100% comfort and sometimes you just must deal with inconveniences like this. 50% (125 votes)

On the final day of the poll I just managed to squeak by and win the poll by two votes! A couple of people claimed that they tried voting more than once and everything like that though, so it might not have been accurate, but the main point was that it was dead 50-50 split basically. I had gone into the poll assuming that everybody would take bathroom access at a job as a basic given, but it turned out that more than half of people didn't seem to think that a woman was entitled to have a bathroom at work in all circumstances.

Perhaps I shouldn't have found that extremely shocking as I did post this poll primarily in omorashi communities. I told people to vote what they felt was right morally speaking, not what they felt was the most entertaining, but of course people don't always follow their conscience. Even a couple of people who voted in the poll told me that yeah it's probably cruel that you don't have a bathroom all day, but hey a woman without a bathroom all day is a pretty entertaining situation to witness! So yes a lot of people who voted admitted that they did kind of actually feel it was wrong but at the same time they would kind of like to see it happen, because when it's happening to somebody else of course is always a lot more entertaining.

I would almost agree with people if it wasn't for the fact that I was that woman who was being denied access to a bathroom! So in a bit of overwhelming irony I, who has written numerous books and stories about women being denied access to a toilet or stuck in situations where they are desperate to pee, was now going to find myself in a situation where I was regularly denied access to a toilet and stuck desperate at work and holding it all the time, and most of the people that I knew in the omorashi community were going to find that very very entertaining while I going to be finding it very very frustrating!

I don't want to go on and on about my experiences at work, because believe me that's going to be a book that's going to be a lot longer than this, a full-length memoir that I am already working the title with so far as being Woman Desperately Seeking Toilet in Times of Covid! So there is another book that you can look forward to, my first work of omorashi nonfiction. I can honestly say that one year ago if you had told me I would be writing a nonfiction book about my omorashi experiences at work I never would have believed you, but after nearly a year of this I have to say it has been a real crazy ride in a really crazy time.

In this book in particular I didn't really address Covid at all because that was sort of not the focus of the book. My real life experiences are directly influenced by Covid in a way that the experiences of the character based off of me in the book are not, but it's interesting that I sort of wrote this book prior to having my job as a way of trying to cope with what it was going to be like and imagine what it was going to be like.

It actually is rather strange as it turned out I was really very accurate predicting other people's reactions. Again the situation was entirely different seeing as my job involves being outdoors and in the field away from toilets or where public toilets are locked, where as in this novel my character works at a job where she is stuck in a warehouse where they don't provide a bathroom all day and circumstances just keep conspiring to keep her from being able to relieve herself.

The similarities however are I ultimately ended up having to hold it about the same length of time that she does through the duration of the day in the novel, which I never would have thought possible for me to do so, and my characters friends in the book, who are based off of my friends in the omorashi community that I have talked online with for numerous years, reacted pretty much the same way as their fictional character counterparts when they found that I actually did get the job, almost down to a T. It really was astonishing how much life imitated art, and looking back a year now I can honestly say that I was accurately predicting my future circumstance as being forced to become one of those women that I had once mocked, women without bathroom access at work. Trust me it's no longer quite as funny as it seemed back when it wasn't me whose bladder was being thrust through the reaping machine!

Since the time of getting my job I actually wrote another book that I have to get around to reading and editing and publishing called The Desperate Girl at the Photo Booth, which is also about a woman at a job without a bathroom but it was written after I had had my job. Looking at those two books it's an interesting time capsule because you can see that this book is sort of the book that I wrote in anticipation of predicting what my job was going to be like, and the other one was written in the aftermath of having had that experience of prolonged toilet deprivation for a while.

Again I don't want to talk too much about my real life job in this book because like I said I'm going to write an entire memoir about that, except I don't know where to start and begin it seeing as it looks like, much to my great misfortune, that this is probably going to be my job for some time to come, and that as long as Covid is still maintaining a problem of closing public restrooms I am going to continue to be in a really desperate situation for the foreseeable future just like the character in this novel.

Needless to say it has been a long, weird and very frustrating journey and the way life has imitated art and vice versa has certainly been interesting, but I never thought that I would become the character in this novel, and yet I totally have in every way, shape and form, and I have to say I would have rather this have remained in entirely fictional situation that I wrote about from a fictional standpoint and not from personal experience, and yet I somehow managed to predict how it was except for the fact that it's just so much worse when it's real. I suppose on one positive level though is that I learned my bladder capacity is much higher than I thought it was, but I would have much rather been able to stay at home with my toilet and not have to learn that very painful and uncomfortable lesson that the gods of karma and desperation had laid out for me.

Once again I could go on and on about this but I have a whole other book to do that, so I will simply conclude by saying I hope that you enjoyed reading this book as much as I enjoyed writing it, as much as I feared living it, and as much as now that I have lived it I wish I hadn't! But I'll say, at least now I am writing from personal experience rather from the ivory tower, or maybe I should be saying from the porcelain throne, of somebody at home always had the never fully appreciated privilege of instantaneous bathroom access on demand whenever I happened to need it. Denial of access to a bathroom seems like an amusing thing until it happens to you. Just keep that in mind, as you never know what karma has in store for you, because the last laugh may very well be on you, as it was in my case and could someday be for you as well.

I suppose that's all I have to say about the development of this novel but I hope that you enjoyed it, and I hope that you will give it a good rating on Amazon and Goodreads. I also hope that you will also do likewise for my other female desperation themed books, The Great Locked Ladies Room Caper, The Terrible, Horrible, No Good Very Desperate Bus Ride and An Aura of Desperation. You can see previews from this book and others, as well as lots of personal accounts of my own desperate experiences and fictional short stories about desperation and all things bathroom related at my original blog at https://desperatejill.livejournal.com/ and my new blog at https://desperatejill83.livejournal.com/.

www.ingramcontent.com/pod-product-compliance
Lightning Source LLC
Chambersburg PA
CBHW072055150726
47999CB00005B/1788